THE GREEK GOD TABLOIDS

RYAN ΩMEGA

The Greek God Tabloids. Copyright © 2008 by Ryan Omega.

All rights reserved. No part of this publication may be reproduced, stored in a retrieval system or transmitted by any means, electronic, mechanical, photocopy, recording or otherwise, without the prior permission of the publisher, except as provided by USA copyright law and brief quotations embodied in literary articles and reviews.

Book design by Ryan Omega

Photography by Alvaro Alvarenga

Models: Alexander Ward, John Basset, Calee Gilliland, Frankie DePriest, Kari Swanson, Dean Flagg

Printed in the United States of America

First Printing: September 2008

This printing: August 2014

ISBN: 978-0-615-25154-7

For Sypher and Hurry Up and Wait.

Special thanks to Rachel Judd for being my second set of eyes.

Hello Morgan and Calvin!

150

Table of Contents

150

PREFACE

I came across all these notes that Dad wrote down from his travels on the various impressions people on Earth had of Olympus and its residents.

Like this one:

"Zeus had a headache. Hermes suggested that Hephaestus take a hammer and chisel to his skull. Hephaestus cracked open his head and out sprung Athene, a full grown adult with a spear and shining armor."

There is so much that is wrong with this. I wonder if my boss had ever read that.

150

Or this one:

"Upon hearing the prophecy, Kronos devoured his children whole so that none would overthrow him."

What is WRONG with these people?

Then we have:

"After letting out all the evils into the world, Pandora closed the box, managing to keep Hope within it."

What happened was not even close.

Somewhere between here in Olympus and Earth, these stories were either tossed into one of Dionysus' orgies or censored and cleaned up by Apollo.

In between assignments that Athene hands to me, I am going to straighten a few of these rumors out. This is going to be a personal project in the hopes that if people on Earth are going to talk about us, they might as well get it right.

These stories have to be better than:

"After Zeus destroyed his father, Kronos, he castrated his penis and threw it into the sea. Within the blood and sea foam, Aphrodite was born."

I'm not touching that one.

Bellaramon

Son of Hermes and child of Demeter

Olympian Department of Justice

Internal Affairs

How Olympus came to be

(Disclaimer: I wasn't here at the beginning of Olympus. Even if I was, I would look pretty damn good for my age.)

Once there was nothing. Just pink clouds and floating streams of light drifting in empty space. It was a newly created world. The streams of light became stars; and the grasses, trees and dirt floated in clumps. There was no order, just pieces of these things that could be used to make a sanctuary or a home. Emerging from another world called "Elsewhere" stepped a woman we all knew as Gaia. She pulled land together with gentle ropes made of flowers and leaves. She was the one responsible for putting all this land and grass into the ground and for putting the pink skies and clouds above. This way, we all have somewhere to walk steadily and sleep.

Gaia was the first ruler of Olympus. She wanted no one to ever have wanted for anything, so she created bounty for everyone. There was an abundance of things to eat, from oxen in the fields, apples in the tree, and fish in the sea. But despite this abundance, mortals are mortals and they have greed. They fight despite that there is plenty to share. They are mean-spirited and harsh and sometimes they kill because they want more. Even if there is plenty, they still want more. Still, no one on Earth knew of the gods in Olympus.

But Olympus had its share of pettiness as well. The Titans were always with competition with each other. Someone had to be the prettiest. Someone had to be the strongest. Being the ruler meant that Gaia needed others to command, but they could not hear her above their own personal contests of pride. Even with Gaia as the creator of the world and of Olympus, those she commanded would tear Olympus apart.

As Olympus began to lose order, Gaia created someone else who can do this by combining parts of darkness and light. This became Gaia's husband, Ouranos. Ouranos could be mean when he wanted, but he was more often firm than cruel. But it was important that he could be more firm than Gaia, who could think only of creating. She allowed her husband to rule while she continued to create the order of Olympus. Ouranos, her beloved, was there to enforce the structure by punishing those who acted without control.

Gaia and Ouranos created many children, each with one part creation and one part order to expand the Universe. Over time Ouranos was succeeded by one of his sons, whose name has been obscured by time. But I shall call him "M" for now. To continue his Father's rule, "M" was also in charge of enforcing the order. However, M was more severe in his measures than his father. To enforce the order, he did not

150

enlist just the normal gods of Olympus. He had hordes of terrifying monsters created to strike fear into obedience. And yes, he succeeded. He made mortals afraid of the uncertain and the unknown. But he also made the gods work for what they have; since the monsters were not relegated to the mortals of Earth, the gods had to fight for their place, too.

By governing this way, the inevitable finally happened - the monsters began to get out of hand. M ruled so tightly that he had created perfect order. But this perfect order came at the price of freedom and for gods and mortals alike, this had become unacceptable.

One grandchild of Ouranos could not stand by and allow this to continue any longer. Olympus and earth had become the playground and battleground of monsters everywhere. Bodies blended into the landscape of the world and daytime was no different from nightmare. So from the depths of Olympus, forgotten because he had made himself scarce, the man known as Kronos stepped forward and led the rebellion.

Kronos waited for a very long time, studying each monster for weakness and each of M's guardians for power. Although many were eager to change the course of tyranny, Kronos always said, "Not yet, not yet." He was waiting for the right sign, even though his followers were losing faith and patience. One day, he looked up to the sky and he saw that the pink skies of Olympus had turned gray and believed that even Olympus, as if it were a living being, was suffering. Even M's own guardians saw the omen in the sky and knew. When Kronos pressed forward against M, they did not stop him. Others stood behind Kronos, if only to see what confrontation occurred.

Kronos sharpened the bones of his hands into long claws, walked up to M and demanded that he vacate the throne. When M snapped his fingers, none of his guardians moved. However, the guardians were unable to move, Kronos had slowed down time so much that they appeared to be still. Kronos took a couple of steps forward and with one swipe of his hand and beheaded M. The rest of the body collapsed to the floor and upon impact, vaporized into a cloud of dark red smoke that seeped into the floor. Olympus began to rain, as if relieved of burden and the skies went from gray to pink was they once were.

Kronos ruled for a while, but he was more of a military general rather than one suited to rule who believed his throne would be any rock whereupon he sat. Whenever his advisors would gather together, his governing seat was always empty because he would be wandering Olympus, surveying it for dangers. Without Kronos there, too many other Titans argued that we needed another ruler and scheming began again for the throne. So Kronos' advisors appointed someone who would take over the responsibility of Olympus while Kronos was away. There was only one deity whom they could all agree to set the mantle of leadership upon: The oldest daughter of Kronos, Demeter, who was wise and diplomatic enough to keep all Gods and Titans from total war. This was a decision made tenuously; she was the only person whom all the Elders did not dislike.

Then one night, when the sun barely edged out the darkness, Kronos received a prophecy: One of his own children would overthrow and kill him. Acting on this prophecy, he imprisoned his own full-grown children in a very deep cavern in the Underworld. And there he kept the six children born to Kronos and Rhea: Demeter, Poseidon, Hestia, Hades, Hera and Zeus. Kronos did not kill them because he could not prove it. Growing more and more afraid of being overthrown, Kronos started to act as if everyone were scheming against him and began to tighten his fist around those he ruled. The monsters he once sealed under the reign of M, he released back into the world to serve him and enforce his will.
150

Rhea, the wife of Kronos, could not stand to see anymore of this tyranny, and began to work against him. She managed to get the key to the prison in the deep cavern, secretly gave it to Zeus and promptly disappeared so that no would ever discover her-treason. She left her children's destiny in their own hands.

Zeus promptly took advantage of the kindness and opened the prison cell, releasing all his siblings. Then mighty Zeus formed a rebellion, the same way Kronos had formed his own rebellion, and led an army against the monsters of his Father. In the end, he slew his own Father, thus fulfilling the prophecy. Demeter ceded the rule of Olympus to Zeus and decided to leave the politics of Olympus behind, choosing to live on Earth among no gods.

Zeus has sat on the high throne of Olympus, overlooking the realm, ever since.

THE PANTHEON (AS I KNOW THEM)

Here in the Olympian Department of Justice, we are required to have dossiers on everyone who is in any kind of position of power, including the Royals like King Zeus and Queen Hera. But if you look in the files, those passages are superficial at best. Hermes' notes from the people on Earth for instance, often refer to my boss as "gray-eyed Athene."

Well, Hera has wide feet. That still does not tell me anything about her and I do not describe her as "stable-footed Hera."

There are Fourteen Olympians whose names come up in the course of the day because when we don't have our normal lives to talk about, we need to talk about someone else. The way I see it, if you're going to talk about someone else, at least get your facts straight.

150

Zeus

Zeus is the current ruler of Olympus. He is often given high regard for his wisdom, but that comes with the knowledge that he has a metal fist he uses to back his rule. Zeus was the youngest, most ambitious of all the siblings and he managed to escape to overthrow Kronos. To secure Olympus from chaos, Zeus appoints his own relatives as administrators, which is why he entrusted Poseidon to handle the ocean and Hades-to deal with the Underworld. When Zeus is not overseeing the security of the kingdom, he spends his time satisfying his endless sex drive with nearly anything that moves. Except his wife.

Hera

Hera is the Queen of Olympus. Her marriage to Zeus was purely a political alliance and completely loveless... especially since Hera is Zeus's older sister (yet they have two or three children). Hera's feels her power is constantly threatened by Zeus's affairs, worried that any of those women or the heirs they might bear could quickly replace her, especially since Hera is not Zeus's first wife (that honor belongs to Themis, whose marriage to the King of Olympus was dissolved when Zeus's father imprisoned him). Hence Hera pursues other women and their children with swift and legendary jealousy. She is to be treated with a respect due a Queen. And she will never let you forget this.

Poseidon

Poseidon is one of Zeus's older brothers, given charge of the seas. Knowing that Poseidon's mood came in one of two flavors: generous or wrathful, Zeus put Poseidon in charge of the waters, which gave him ample room to do as he wished. Although also known for a sex drive (which will explain why ocean waters are so frothy), his creativity is severely underestimated. Looking at the sea creatures alone would show how expansive his canvas is. Of all Zeus's brothers and sisters,

Poseidon is the most stubborn, willing to hold a grudge for eons. At best, you can only make a truce with one of Poseidon's infamous grudges, rather than end one.

Hades

Hades, who is quite sensitive, is another one of Zeus's older brothers and was forced to handle the Underworld under the threat of Zeus. Staying in the Underworld with the restless spirits of the dead led Hades to become more depressed, some might even say whiny. The longer he dwelt in the Underworld, his skin became more pale until it resembled that of his subjects. Hades was at least smart enough to delegate most of his unpleasant work to other people. It wasn't until he took Demeter's daughter, Persephone, as a wife that he began to be much happier. Even though he is invited to many functions, his introversion keeps him in the Underworld. Despite the gloom, it is at least comfortable for him.

Demeter

Demeter is Zeus's oldest sister and a nurturer at heart. Before her imprisonment by her father, she was left in charge of Olympus when Kronos went missing for extended periods of time. Demeter was the only one that the Titans would allow to hold the throne since she could handle things with great diplomacy. But the incredible amount of politicking required to stay in power burned her out. When Zeus took the throne, Demeter moved to Earth and left the politics of Olympus behind. Her relocation to Earth increased her influence over the world, so the land is very much affected by her mood. Most art depicts her as a young maiden, but she is more a full figured, wide-hipped and big-breasted mother. (I should know this. She happens to be my mother and I could never have asked for better)

Hestia

Hestia is another one of Zeus's siblings. When Zeus asked her to handle administrative duties in his kingdom, she outright refused an was the only one to do so. She is more of a socialite who would rather drink tea and gossip over events in Olympus. As a result, she is the most well informed person in all of Olympus, especially when it comes to scandals. She knows who is having an affair with whom, who owes political favors to who, and is skillful enough to keep herself above the entire fray and out of the rumor mill. Hestia abstains from alcohol and sex - not simply because she is prudish. She knows full well that either of those-indulgences can lead to someone taking advantage of her... and she would rather have all those advantages to herself.

Athene

Athene is a daughter of Zeus, known for her wide body of knowledge and wisdom. (I have to say that because I work for her, but she is a fair boss.) She thinks very much like her father; so when Zeus cannot think very clearly, she is the first person Zeus consults. In fact, it would be fair to say that while Hera is the Queen, Athene would be considered second-in-command of Olympus. When Athene is not handling official bureaucratic matters on behalf of her father, she loves mental games and puzzles. Unfortunately, this also means she thinks of war as a cerebral challenge rather than physical battle so when conflict breaks out, she thinks in terms of numbers and calculations and not people with casualties. In Olympus, she is charged with dispensing Olympian justice, which looks nothing like justice on Earth. Law is only considered in Olympus as strong as those who have power to enforce it, not viewed as the protection for the common good. Athene is keenly aware of this and uses all the political power she has to keep the entirety of Olympus in check.

Hermes

Hermes is a son of Zeus, and the fastest, most versatile, and most athletic of the gods in Olympus. As someone with high energy, cunning smarts (rather than Athene's brand of wisdom) and an inventive nature, he can get several things done in just one day that would take others at least a week to accomplish. Also, Hermes believes in working smarter not harder, so he will always be able to find time for parties and debauchery. He is not above playing practical jokes on others, including seeing what he can get away with. Hermes boasts one of the best bodies on Olympus, not in the least a particular appendage hanging below his waist, rumors of which ensure Hermes a permanent invitation to all the best debaucheries. For all the trickery and mess that he can get into, people find he is the hardest to blackmail; Hermes is not known for his shame.

This man happens to be my father. Before I found out, he preferred me to call him "Uncle" whenever he came to visit. This might give you an idea of what kind of father he was.

Apollo

Apollo is the son of Zeus and Leto, praised as one of the most learned men in Olympus. He is the ideal when it comes to physical appearance, brains, creativity and power. For all that, he has yet to have any kind of stable relationship with anyone on Olympus. He is fairly unlucky when it comes to women: they either run away from him or leave the next day. As a man who is very much into women, men who approach him sexually unnerve him; unfortunately, Apollo's never ending frustration is the fact that his "prettiness" attracts more men than women. Apollo finds he's often at odds with Hermes, thinking Hermes' kind of learning a bit barbaric while Hermes finds Apollo's opinions stuffy. Apollo rides the sun chariot to guarantee the daylight to the world.

150

Artemis

Artemis is Apollo's twin sister who is very much into the hunt and the woods. AND women. Artemis is incredibly territorial and usually solitary. It does not mean that she isn't friendly or feminine. In fact, most men are not aware she is inclined towards women until they make sexual advances towards her and find those advances are unwanted... with a quick arrow to the thigh of the offender. Artemis is the biggest defender of wildlife among Olympus and as mistress of the hunt, she would never endanger the balance of predators and prey in the forests that she protects. Artemis rides the moon chariot, partly because of duty and partly because the hunt is more challenging and exciting at night.

Ares

Ares, the first born son of King Zeus and Queen Hera is the resident bad boy of Olympus. As the son of the King and Queen, he can come across as spoiled because he can get away with many things that would earn other deities a thunderbolt to the face. He's not ashamed to be a known troublemaker. Between his parents, Zeus expects Hera to parent him and Hera expects Zeus to parent him. Thus, no one really tells him what to do, even when he can get violent or out of control. Surprisingly, when you first meet Ares, you meet someone who is quite handsome and has presence... until he opens his mouth. He is often a participant in war rather than a strategist and is first to get into a fight. Olympus is hopeful that he will grow out of this rebellious phase... eventually.

Hephaestus

Hephaestus is the second born son of King Zeus and Queen Hera. When he was born, he was deformed and Zeus tossed him out of Olympus into the ocean because he assumed that the baby was some kind of cruel joke. Zeus reluctantly accepted him back, whereupon it turned out that Hephaestus was good-natured and skilled at metalwork. After his marriage to Aphrodite, he was encouraged to grow a beard to hide his facial deformity. He grew in size while lifting very heavy pieces of metal on a daily basis, giving him a very stocky and barrel-chested appearance. Hephaestus is a continual optimist and his fellow Olympians find little reason to get onto his bad side, if he has one.

Aphrodite

Aphrodite is the child of Zeus and Dione... even though legends suggest she was Kronos' castrated penis turned into a woman and born from the frothy sea. That's a very exaggerated and suggestive metaphor yet not completely inaccurate. Even though she is known for her sexual wiles, she is somehow not brazen or classless about it. And for all of her open sexuality, she does not have a remote interest in women. She isn't against it; women just don't appeal to her in that way. She may seem superficial and vain, and people would be right about that. Her philosophy is that people can't have relationships if they make no effort to present themselves well. She likes to play matchmaker and it gives her a high to get people together. But Aphrodite is not known for her foresight; she still likes to match people even if they are not compatible as long as their affair will amuse her.

Dionysus

Dionysus is a son of Zeus and a mortal princess, Semele. His reputation is legendary for throwing the most lavish and famous (or infamous) parties in all of Olympus and Earth. He will often enhance the atmosphere with wines and other substances so more than a few gods, people and others have been conceived at his parties. People have cut off their right foot to get into his exclusive parties and brag about walking funny the next day. Dionysus has managed to gain an extensive amount of social influence to the point of being a trendsetter. However, he never claims any responsibility for any of the aftermath his events cause. At times, he is

150

known to use fits of ecstasy and passion to get people to agree to oaths that they would never swear when sober. With the exception of those related to the royal family in Olympus, anyone found to be on Dionysus' "outcast list" will find their social lives to be worse than Hera's banishment or Zeus' thunderbolts.

This list is not exhaustive of all the gods that hold power in Olympus; these happen to be the most recognizable. They also would be more likely to be offended if you don't talk about them at all than if you did so disparagingly.

Some guy named Prometheus

Prometheus is considered mankind's greatest hero because he brought man fire. His punishment was to be chained to a rock with a vulture that would eat out his liver.

And yet... the Prometheus I knew did not actually mean to be a hero. He simply wanted glory. It just so happened that all he benefited man.

It is important to note that Prometheus was a Titan. When Zeus became the ruler of all Olympus, the Titans had two choices. They could either cooperate with Zeus's new rule or continue to war against him. Prometheus believed in a third option: subverting his rule.

Prometheus pledged his loyalty to Zeus very publicly so that he could trick Zeus into having no doubts. Zeus doubted people who made such a grand show of

150

loyalty and briefly turned his attention from Olympus to Earth. At this time, despite that Gaia created the Earth and gave a home to creatures, it was littered with formless beings. They had limbs and a mouth but no eyes or speech. Zeus pointed down and asked Prometheus to make them honor him.

No one had ever made real contact with the world. Because the world looked so dark, Prometheus brought a torch of fire with him. As he passed the clouds in the sky that separated Olympus from the Earth, he found that there were people were not very different from that within Olympus; except these people did not have the powers of gods or titans. Upon closer inspection, they had faces and were not animals. When they saw the fire, they appeared to open their eyes and saw Prometheus. Immediately, they knew they beheld a god and treated him as one.

Prometheus went back to Earth several times to spread his teachings, in return the people revered and worshiped him. Prometheus enjoyed the attention, and when they asked about what was in the sky, he talked nothing about the others in Olympus. He told them that he was the only god.

In the meantime, Zeus was impressed with Prometheus' work: People who were once savages had become cultured; and Prometheus made it sound like he was getting the people to accept the majesty of Zeus. Zeus was excited to visit the people on Earth. Prometheus, who was enamored of the people loving and adoring him, had no desire for Zeus to mess up his little playground of followers.

In a rush, Prometheus decided to go to the people and warn them of nightmares and terrible day visions that they will have. He told them they would see a very old man who believed he was god of the world, but was delusional. Prometheus told them to "play along" as if this old man was a god, for making him angry would upset him and bring about harsh destruction.

The next day, Zeus went down to Earth expecting to be received in grand style. But such was his expectation that he brought all the other gods along with him. With all the gods present, Prometheus felt ill. He did not expect anyone but Zeus to arrive. As a result, the mortals on Earth were introduced to several gods at once. They began to learn their names and know what guidance they can bring. The people expected to see a delusional old man, but when Zeus appeared, he presented himself as a charismatic wizened elder.

Prometheus attempted to run away, but it did not take long for Zeus to find him. Zeus charged Prometheus to with treason against Olympus and decided death was too good for him. Instead, Zeus chained him to a public rock and had a vulture feast upon his liver while Prometheus was still alive. At night, the liver would regenerate, only to be torn out by the same vulture the next morning. The punishment was quite public so no other Titan would forget.

No Titan ever decided to challenge Zeus's rule again. Outwardly, of course.

THE BIRTH OF ATHENE

Rumor has it on Earth that people widely believed that when Athene was born, she started off as a headache in Zeus's skull. Hephaestus grabbed his hammer and chisel and broke open Zeus's skull and Athene was born a full adult, wearing a spear, shield and full plate of armor. But seriously, let's not even contemplate the physical impossibility of that, let alone thinking that the king of all of Olympus had reproductive organs implanted somewhere in his skull compressed against his brain.

Athene being born as a full is but a metaphor. That's not how it actually happened.

She had a mother herself, the daughter of the Titan Oceanus by the name of Metis. The rumor persisted that Zeus swallowed Metis and suddenly, his skull became pregnant with Athene.

The truth is uninteresting, probably a bit depressing. I'm not sure where people got the idea of Metis being swallowed, but I'm guessing it alluded to some sexual act that I'm not going into at the moment. However, what is significant is that shortly after Metis gave birth to Athene, she died. For some reason, the immortality promised to all the gods was not given to her.

Without a mother, Zeus raised Athene as his own and paid special attention to her. I am not sure why Zeus did not abandon her when he often abandons his other children. Rumor has Zeus saw Metis die in childbirth, but only the Fates really know the truth.

The special attention had an impact on Athene. She was very keen and smart from a young age. She was acting more like an adult and at age five, she held perfectly normal and intelligent conversations with other adults. At the same time, she took after her father mentally. Athene very often thought like her father when it came to rational thinking. Most of all, Athene and Zeus were very matched with regards to military strategy. Still, knowing Athene, she always wondered how different her life would be with a mother.

The only part where she and her father differ significantly is that of sex. Zeus was quick to pursue passionate couplings and put out the flames of his loins. Athene was not. But as far as the blood goes, Athene did have stirrings that needed to be quenched...

Keep in mind that Athene was a sensible woman. She would not allow her raging hormones to dictate how she would behave. In fact, she once told me that she used to have menstrual cycles that would affect her. Then one day, she was tired of being so irrational so she meditated upon them to stop. Now, she has no menstrual cycle... according to her anyway.

And Athene knows that if she did not receive satisfaction every so often, it would affect her ability to perform her tasks. So for the sake of her work, she does have a lover to service her as needed. It's very much done in a business-like manner, like visiting a physician. She gets the services she needs and goes on her way.

Athene is presumed to be a virgin goddess simply because people have never seen her in a relationship. But Athene views it as a state of a body rather than a condition for purity.

150

Besides, her view of "Virginity" is probably one that most would not expect: "What's the point of keeping a present if you cannot open it?"

That reminds me… it's time to disrobe and attend to Athene. Excuse me.

Hades and Persephone

As I understand it, this all started with Hades' constant complaining about his lot in life. His lot was to deal with the Underworld and he constantly felt miserable. I imagine that dealing with dead people all the time with severed body parts and diseased flesh is no boost to a positive attitude. But after a while, he was complaining about being lonely... and he would do this ALL the time.

Hades would complain so often it irritated Zeus. Zeus kept telling him to go find a girl and get laid so he could feel better. I'm not sure if he tried or not, but his mood did not change. Hades wanted romance and without it, he just seemed miserable all the time.

Eventually, Zeus got so aggravated he decided to be proactive about it. He got his daughter, Aphrodite, to create a magic black flower Hades could use to lure

150

and seduce any woman he liked. I'm assuming that it works on men as well, but Hades was never really into them.

When Hades received the flower he was overjoyed at first, but then something entered his mind. How did he know his intended would stay with him forever? Zeus and Aphrodite looked at each other not sure what to say, but when Hades asked Zeus to swear onto the River Styx that whomever he used the flower on would be his forever, things began to get a bit uncomfortable.

"There are no guarantees in life, not even in love," said Aphrodite, but Hades was deaf to this. Zeus believed if this issue were not resolved now, he would never hear the end of it.

"This is not something that can be sworn by the River Styx," said Zeus. "You cannot do that with love."

"You do it all the time," retorted Hades.

"With mortals, yes. But this rule does not apply to gods."

Hades walked away in a slump. But Aphrodite could not bear to see her uncle looking so defeated and rushed to his side.

"Uncle," she said, "Life has no guarantees, but we can devise things by contract. Like marriage."

"How?" asked Zeus, overhearing with a sudden interest.

"This black flower can only seduce, but it will not keep her here forever," said Aphrodite to Hades. "It will only use magic to make her to see your good intentions. That is all this flower will do. If she cares for you, she will partake of your food. A woman who despises you will have no appetite."

Hades said, "I am not looking for someone who could despise me--'

"Well, do you want a girl or not?!" bellowed Zeus who was getting fed up. "Brother, my daughter is giving you a solution. I would have thought that you, knowing protocol, would accept her good graces and get to it!"

Hades could not look at Zeus's face. Only his feet.

Zeus sighed. "I am not going to overrule my daughter in this. I cannot force anyone to love you, no matter how much you want it. I can only bind them to you. I hope for the sake of all Olympus that you have bound someone who does like you. Now take the flower and go. And for the sake of all Olympus, make sure whoever you choose likes you!"

So with that, Hades took the flower and looked far and wide for *the* woman. One day, he came stumbling onto a grassy knoll while a group of beautiful young women picked flowers for a festival. One young girl stood out among them. It happened to be my sister, Persephone. He planted the flower nearby a group of spring blossoms. The flower itself stood out because it was black, unlike all the other flowers in the area.

Persephone could smell the flower before she saw it. She wandered off by herself and saw the black flower. She admired its fragrance and its beauty. When she stooped over to pick it up, the earth opened beneath her feet. As the earth began to swallow her up, Persephone fainted and Hades caught her in his arms while driving a chariot and took her to the Underworld.

It was a while before her playmates realized Persephone had vanished. When they could not find her, then ran to my mother, Demeter, and told her she was missing. My mother panicked and immediately left to go to High Olympus to find Zeus.

Mother still held a considerable amount of power at the time. Before Zeus came to rule in Olympus, she had actually held the throne over Olympus. When she arrived in High Olympus, people cleared their way for her as she charged up to find Zeus. She stormed the throne room.

"Where is my daughter?" she demanded of Zeus.

"How would I know where your daughter is?" asked Zeus. "She never leaves your land. None of your children do."

150

"She is not there anymore!" she cried, with tears rolling down her face. "I demand to know where she is!" From what I understand, Zeus was about to tell her off, but Hera grabbed his arm, shook her head and motioned for him to calm down. Zeus composed himself, closed his eyes and concentrated. From here I can only speculate he figured out Persephone was the one Hades had chosen, and now he had to figure out how to break it to her.

"She is with Hades," said Zeus. "She is safe."

My mother cried with relief. "Thank goodness, I will go see her."

"Ah--- I will go with you," said Zeus, still trying to figure out how to break this to her gently. "She is my daughter; I want to know this, too."

Zeus and Demeter traveled to the Underworld together where they were greeted by Hades, who wore a smile that never left his face. They asked where Persephone was, and he said she was in his bedroom. I do not want to think about the look on my mother's face at this point. But from what I understand, Hades assured my mother nothing had happened. "She needed a place to rest," he said. "My bed is the most comfortable place down here."

"Can I see her?" asked my mother.

"Of course---"

"What are you doing?" demanded Zeus, grabbing Hades' arm.

"'I'm allowing Demeter to go see her daughter...'

"No, no... you should get her yourself and bring her out here... going to your room is very inappropriate," Zeus insisted.

Hades shrugged and left to go retrieve Persephone from his room.

While Hades was away, Zeus gave the bad news to Demeter. "My dear sister, Demeter. There is something I need you to know. Persephone no longer belongs to you."

For a moment, Demeter stopped the world to hear his words. "What do you mean... she no longer belongs to me?"

"There is a contract I have to uphold. Hades wants a wife.... and it appears he has picked your daughter."

"But... but..." my mother was stunned that Zeus would have done this behind her back. "But no! I have not consented! She is MY daughter!"

"She is my daughter, too, Demeter. And I gave my consent. "

"Zeus! How dare you! You wicked man! You gave up our daughter without even telling me? How could you do that?"

"It is for the best, Demeter!'" he roared at her.

"Oh no, it is not!" said my mother and she ran towards Hades' room. When Demeter ran into the bedroom, she saw Persephone contently eating from a plate of fruit. In her hand was a pomegranate.

Demeter, looked at her in amazement. "Did you--" asked Demeter, and when she saw six chewed pomegranate seeds in her hand, my mother figured out what happened. Hades and Persephone were "married." The pomegranate was their "contract." But when she looked at Persephone, Persephone did not seem upset at all. In fact, she was very happy.

Zeus told Demeter it was important for Persephone to be with her husband now. So Zeus enforced this by disallowing my mother to see Persephone until Spring. As a result, my mother went through depressions and it would be evident on Earth, affecting the seasons.

When I asked Persephone later why she liked Hades, she went on and on about how kind, nice and gentle he was, not to mention very handsome and devoted. Unlike every other god in Olympus, Hades remains completely monogamous. The "proposal" was not exactly the best of circumstances but the marriage turned out better than anyone could have expected.

150

PANDORA'S NOT SO SMALL BOX

First of all, yes, there was a Pandora. Sort of.

Yes, there was a box. Sort of.

However, "Pandora" was never married off to the Titan Epimetheus, the dumber brother of Prometheus. Pandora was never fashioned out of clay by Hephaestus. Pandora was not the first mortal woman on Olympus.

The truth is Pandora was a fictitious name used by a woman whose true identity has been lost to time. She went by several other names but the name "Pandora" stuck because it means "gift to all." And many people think the box was this small jewelry box that fits in the palm of her hand. It was closer in size to a large trunk. A VERY large trunk.

Inside Pandora's box were the fruits of all her evil. She kept the bones of all the men she had murdered in that very large box. She was just a woman whose reprehensible actions would be remembered forever.

Pandora was a woman who killed men for sport. Often, she would marry them and dispose of them on their wedding night. When relatives of the victims or guards would try to find her, they would find no trace of her at all.

Pandora was very ambitious and she would set her sights on some of the most powerful men on Earth. She drove fear into the hearts of men. She in fact drove men to become more faithful to their female companions.

That was, until she decided to marry a powerful man she did not realize was a god. There were rumors it had been Apollo or Ares, but it was never clear which god she had married. When confronted with the rumor, Apollo and Ares would both just smile and walk away.

On her wedding night with this god, she waited until he was sleeping before she stabbed him in the heart. But as soon as she drew her weapon back, the god woke up and revealed his full majestic glory to her. Since no mortal can withstand a god in full glory, she burned up and died from the exposure.

Many have asked, "How is it that such a story eventually became a story of a woman who received a box of evils, opened them and released them to the world?"

The answer is simple: Because in a world ruled by men, men can't have that kind of fear running around. Instead of making 'Pandora' the most feared killer in history, mortal men have made her the biggest scapegoat. And in turn, have made her deeds the fault of all women.

So as each generation tells the story, the story becomes less about a cruel woman and becomes more about a woman of insatiable curiosity. The box in each generation becomes smaller and smaller and the contents become more unreal.

In the end, some storyteller decided to add hope where there was none.

And thus shut the truth of Pandora's box forever.

150

THE MARRIAGE OF ZEUS AND HERA

Zeus, whose libido is as big as his power, has been known to have quite a list of lovers, Each time angering his wife, Hera, in the process. Of course, this begs the question, "If Zeus keeps cheating on his wife all the time, then why did they even get married in the first place?"

The answer is simple: It is a powerful political alliance.

For most people, no one really understood why Zeus would even consider marrying his older sister, Hera. To most gods and nobility, no one marries for love. They marry for the sake of political power and alliance. Zeus and Hera understood this full well when they got married.

Life after overthrowing the old ruler (and Zeus' father), Kronos, was very unstable. Just because Kronos was overthrown did not mean everyone was simply going to obey. As Zeus was powerful and single when he took the throne, the question came up of who would serve as his consort. There was never more scheming than at this time.

Never mind that Zeus had already been married before, to the daughter of Oceanus, Themis. Their relationship had resulted in several children, but when Kronos decided to imprison his own children, Oceanus declared the marriage of his daughter void. There was no point for Themis to be married to a doomed man. Themis accepted her father's wishes and Kronos accepted the separation.

When Zeus finally ascended the Olympian throne, Oceanus thought this would be the perfect time to remind Zeus that Themis was his wife. But the declaration of the marriage-void had been so public that no god or Titan in their right mind would simply let it slide when they had the opportunity to marry into the royalty of Olympus. Zeus was also rather disappointed Themis chose not to stand by him when he was imprisoned, and so taking her back was not desirable.

So while he established his rule of Olympus, he was bombarded with requests from every Titan and god to take his or her daughter into marriage. After a while Zeus asked Poseidon to handle their requests and Poseidon did so gladly, making love to many of the candidates to test them for "worthiness." Then Hestia, one of Zeus's other sisters, decided to intervene and proclaimed she would test the worthiness of each girl without needing them to lie horizontally. Poseidon scowled at her interference but Zeus was willing to hear her out.

The test was simple: Carry an urn of your father's ashes on top of your head from the door of the throne room to the throne and kneel in subservience. Most people thought this was a strange request, but Zeus understood this perfectly. This meant the father of the woman would have to be dead, so his influence would not interfere with Zeus' rule.

Failure to accomplish this strange task would mean death. And so any woman wishing to become the bride of Zeus would first have to travel to the River Styx in the Underworld and leave their immortality behind. Several ambitious women tried at their mother's urging, and all of them have failed. In nervousness,

150

many of them tripped and fallen. Soon, the throne room was stacked high with ashes, those of dead fathers and failed women.

Hestia and Hera mused among themselves. "This test is extremely simple, I am not certain how so many women could have failed," said Hera.

"Maybe you should try this, young sister," suggested Hestia. "Not many women can bear the weight on their shoulders of being queen." Hera was not sure how many would feel about marrying her own brother. Yet this was exactly the suggestion Hera wanted to hear, for she too was politically ambitious.

Hera went to Poseidon and asked of the ashes of her father Kronos that had been dumped into the ocean when he was defeated. Poseidon scooped those ashes for her and placed them in an ivory seashell urn. Hera traveled to the River Styx in the guise of an old woman and left her immortality behind.

Hera appeared before Zeus in the throne room with an urn of her father's ashes on her head. Zeus asked Hera what she was doing. Hera replied she is proving this feat could be done. With the urn on her head, the weight barely weighed her down. There were so many ashes on either side that it became impossible for her to fall. She reached the throne, reached above her head and handed the urn to Zeus. "That task was simple," said Hera.

"This now means you two are meant to be husband and wife," said Hestia and she joined them together at that moment, forming an everlasting alliance that could not be corrupted by another family of gods. Hera reclaimed her immortality and the news spread quickly that Zeus had taken a consort.

Still Themis contested the marriage. "This marriage is no good unless it is consummated and results in an heir," said Themis in a rage. "And Zeus would not be sick enough to have a child with his own sister." Hera, so angered by the challenge of Themis and Zeus, so disgusted by a former wife who simply wanted him for his power went to their marriage bed that night, determined to conceive. Their lovemaking was so angry that the child conceived, Ares, would always have a violent temper as the result of his parents' feelings that night.

With the conditions of the marriage satisfied, Zeus and Hera remained married without any intention of love. Each lover Zeus takes is a threat to Hera's power and Hera continues to punish every lover to make sure no one takes her power away from her.

150

HEPHAESTUS, APHRODITE, AND ARES

Hephaestus had everything going against him. First of all, he had his loveless parents, Zeus and Hera, the king and queen of Olympus. It just so happened that one night, they were so intoxicated and high that Hera became pregnant. When Hera finally gave birth, it was clear the abundant use of wine during her pregnancy had affected the development of her baby. When she saw Hephaestus for the first time, she knew what a horrible thing wine did to a child. He was born lame and his face deformed. Since then, she advised all women carrying children to stay away from wine.

When Zeus beheld his new son, he took one look at him and thought Hephaestus was a cruel joke Hera had played. In anger, he threw him out of Olympus like a discus, wanting the real baby. Hera's jaw dropped and she rushed to grab him as he flew from Zeus' arms. Hera flew to Earth and grabbed the baby before he landed among the jagged rocks of the sea. When Hera returned and explained the baby was not a joke, Zeus was completely embarrassed and promised to take care of him. Reluctantly.

Although Hephaestus was constantly compared unfavorably to his older brother, Ares, his good nature did not let veiled insults or politics hinder him. Ares may have been good-looking and charismatic, but he was also brash, spoiled and caused trouble because he could get away with it. Hephaestus was amused by simple things and friendly to everyone.

It wasn't until he was taught by Hades to work with metals that his true talent began to emerge. His metalcrafts were marked with unsurpassed beauty and his weapons cut so cleanly. When Zeus gave Hephaestus his thunderbolt, which used to look like a slow moving ball of fire, Hephaestus took it to his forge. The result was a thunderbolt with a beautiful jagged edge, which made it as deadly as it was graceful. Since then, Zeus always wanted Hephaestus to work on his thunderbolts.

When the beautiful goddess, Aphrodite, came to live in Olympus, many of the gods fought over her affections. These fights brought instability to Olympus and Zeus wanted to end this by marrying her off. Aphrodite was not really sure who to pick so each one started to hand her gifts. She was showered by gold, statues, jewelry and other trinkets from her suitors. When it was Hephaestus's turn to give her a gift, all the others laughed at him. They said he simply did not have a chance, with his lame body and deformed face. He simply said he had the same chance as everyone else and offered his present to her. It was a magic girdle that would make her so attractive, no man could resist her. In this case, the girdle cinched her waist to make her hips look wider and pushed out her breasts. Aphrodite loved the present and chose him for a husband.

For a while, the marriage was good. But more and more Hephaestus's focus was on his forge rather than his wife. Aphrodite was getting more and more lonely to the point where her own brother, Ares, was looking more and more attractive to her. One night, Hephaestus did not come home and Ares returned from an exercise

150

wearing nothing, muscles glistening with sweat. Aphrodite threw herself at him and they began a torrid affair.

Over time, Aphrodite talked to Hephaestus less and less and Hephaestus suspected Aphrodite was being unfaithful. So he crafted an invisible net that hung over the bed that would trigger when more than one body was on it. When he returned from the forge that night, he found the naked Aphrodite and Ares caught underneath the net in the middle of an adulterous embrace.

Hephaestus grabbed Hermes and Poseidon and showed them the proof of Aphrodite's unfaithfulness. But instead of being angry, Hermes and Poseidon were somewhat turned on by what they saw. The other gods who came in and looked at the spectacle started laughing and joked that Ares was the luckiest man on Olympus.

Hephaestus ran away to his forge, feeling horrible not because everyone laughed at him, but because Aphrodite was not faithful. She went to his forge and pleaded with him to forgive her. She explained her loneliness to her husband. "You cannot have your forge and me as two wives," she said.

Hephaestus understood this was his fault and decided he would work only when he needed to, and spend the rest of his time with her. He forgave her even if she had other lovers. Because even with his simple nature, he knew he was not going to have another woman as beautiful as her.

THE FAVOR OF DEMETRUS

Helios, the Titan of the sun who drove the chariot of fire horses before Apollo did, had numerous children. The only reason why 14 are listed under Helios are because they are the only ones considered to be gods. The first 13 are daughters who are collectively known as the Helionites. And the last of them was a son by the name of Demetrus.

Helios kept his children from the politics of Olympus and provided what he could for them socially. Thus the Helionites were well-bred and well-educated socialites. But for his son, Demetrus, Helios' only aspiration was to take care of his farm. So Demetrus lived a very simple life on the farm and most of his time was being a shepherd to golden sheep.

One day, as Demetrus traveled around the island (because Helios' farm occupied an entire island to itself), he noticed some of the flock were missing. He was not quite sure what had happened and after making calls to the sheep, he got no response. So he went to search for his missing flock.

He found the missing sheep had gathered around something on the beach. When Demetrus came close to that something, he found the body of a man with soggy clothes. Demetrus shook the body and found him alive but weak.

"Water," said the bearded man. "I need water to drink."

Demetrus looked puzzled. "But the ocean is there behind you. That is plenty of water."

"But I need clean water from a well or a spring. Do you have any?" Before Demetrus replied, he rushed to get a bucket of fresh water from a spring and bring it to the seemingly shipwrecked man. After drinking the water, the man looked relieved and suddenly the beard began to disappear and the face because very handsome. The ragged clothes melted away and before him stood none other than Apollo.

"Thank you very much for your kind deed. I am Apollo and I shall perform a favor for you."

Demetrus stood there happy to know the person he rescued was healthy. "You don't owe me any favors," said Demetrus. "It is something people should do anyway."

Apollo looked at him oddly. "But you don't understand. I insist I perform a favor for you. It is my way of repaying you."

"And I am telling you," said Demetrus, " I do not need to be paid back." For Apollo, this was highly unusual. He always paid his debts.

"I can give you anything you want. I can give you money. I can give you women. I can give you treasures and skills beyond what you can imagine. Anything you desire, I will give it."

Demetrus looked at him skeptically. "There is nothing I want. But may I change my mind later?"

"Yes," said Apollo. "You have one day to tell me what it is you want."

Demetrus ran to his father to tell him of the good news and to ask him what he should request. But Helios was at the stables, preparing to leave on his journey into the sky.

"Father!" cried out Demetrus. "I have something to tell you!"

"Can it not wait?" said Helios. "I must be in the sky now because day must come. I must do my duty." Before Demetrus could tell him again, Helios departed.

When it was noon, the sun chariot was high in the sky. Although others feel it is too high to talk to him, this did not stop Demetrus.

"Father!" cried out Demetrus. "I have something to tell you!"

"Can it not wait?" said Helios. "I am very high in the sky and there is nothing I can do now but to come down. I must do my duty." Before Demetrus could tell him again, Helios was avoiding the stardust in the sky.

When it was night and the horses were back in their stables, Demetrus tried again to talk to his father as he was heading to bed.

"Father!" cried out Demetrus. "I have something to tell you!"

"Can it not wait?" said Helios. "It is very late at night and I must get my rest. I must do my duty." Before Demetrus could tell him again, Helios was asleep and no one could wake him.

Demetrus was very sad when he wandered out to the beach. Apollo was there to greet him.

"The time is here," said Apollo. "What is it you want?"

Exasperated but true to his heart, Demetrus cried out, "I wish my father were not so busy to his duty that he cannot make time for me."

Apollo smiled at him and said, "I will grant you this favor. Meet me tomorrow very early because we must talk before you greet your father." With that, Apollo promptly disappeared.

The next morning, Helios was getting ready with his horses when Demetrus approached him.

"Father!" cried out Demetrus. "I have something to tell you!"

"Can it not wait?" said Helios. "I must be in the sky now because day must

150

come. I must do my duty."

"No, it cannot wait," said Demetrus, saying those words for the first time.

Helios stopped himself and looked at him. "What is it, my son?"

"Zeus, the king of gods, wants to talk to you," said Demetrus. Appearing from air, Zeus and Apollo were standing before Helios. Although Helios was much older than either one, he bowed to them because he knew his place.

"Helios," said Zeus, addressing him formally. "I wish to thank you for your service driving this chariot of the sun for so long. But it is time for you to rest."

"I understand," said Helios, resigned without constesting. "But who is to take over the reins?"

"Apollo here shall drive the chariot of the sun until someone more suitable can take his place," said Zeus. Helios handed him the reins and Apollo has been driving the chariot of the sun ever since.

And the favor was granted to Demetrus so he could spend more time with his father.

ATALANTA AND HER GOLDEN APPLES

Atalanta was young girl borne to the king of Arcadia, but because he only wanted boys, he arranged to have Atalanta exposed in the wilderness to die. The king explained to the public the child died at birth, much to the distress of the queen. The queen prayed to Artemis, the goddess of the forests and the hunt, to please spare her only daughter and for her to return to the family safely.

Artemis found the baby in response to the prayer, but knowing the girl's father would simply try another way to get rid of her, Artemis kept Atalanta in the safety of the forest. She had the baby nursed by a mother bear. As Atalanta grew up, she learned to fend for herself and Artemis trained Atalanta in the ways of the hunt and the forest. But Artemis also schooled her so she may not be completely lost when it came to civilization. As a result of Artemis's schooling, Atalanta also picked

150

up Artemis's love of women.

Atalanta grew to be a woman who was as skilled with a bow and arrow as she was beautiful. For the longest time, hunters hunting in her forest would speak of a ravishing maiden who lived in the woods. They figured her for a wood nymph until news came of a savage boar roaming the land. A man named Meleagros formed a war party to destroy this boar that was eating human flesh in Kalydonia. Many men assembled... and then Atalanta appeared. She had a presence about her that made the other men put away any thoughts of laughter and ridicule out of their head.

In the hunt, a couple of boys acted as decoys to get the boar out of a bush; and one young man fell as the boar charged. But Atalanta's arrow was so swift and precise, the arrow drew the first blood, lodged into the boar's right eye. After more attacks, the boar finally collapsed and Atalanta was awarded the boar's skin. However, a couple of men wished to take the boar's skin and glory from Atalanta by force. Meleagros handled this quickly by slaying them.

The next day, word spread far and wide of the "young wood nymph" named Atalanta who drew the first blood of a man-eating boar. This news spread to the Queen of Arcadia, who had long given up hope of her daughter still being alive. She demanded Atalanta be brought to her. Unfortunately, the last three soldiers who were sent to get her never returned; Atlanta sensed their aggression and killed them in self-defense. So the Queen herself went to find her and prayed for the guidance of Artemis. Dangerously alone in the woods at night, the Queen found Atalanta bathing in the river. And when the Queen called out, she knew Atalanta for her own lost daughter.

Atalanta was brought home to a rejoicing father who was proud of her hunting accomplishment. However, he also said it was time for her to wed but Atalanta refused, as she had no interest in men at all. The King insisted, and Atalanta finally decided if a suitor could defeat her in a foot race, then shewould be wed. If a the potential suitor could not defeat her, then she would mark them for death and hunt them down. The terms were not ideal for the King, but he figured someone from his lands should be able to best her in a race. After all, she was only a girl...

Months went by and Atalanta won every single race, besting warriors, soldiers, athletes and others. And Atalanta marked them all for death and struck down every single one. The King was worried that if more people kept challenging her, soon he would have no more army left to defend Arcadia.

One young man by the name of Melanion, who was not very strong nor very fast, could not help but fall in love with Atalanta at first sight. He did not know what to do except to go to the Temple of Aphrodite and pray for assistance. He was told to open his hands as he closed his eyes. When he opened his hands, there he held three golden apples. "You will know what to do with these," said Aphrodite in a vision.

And so Melanion challenged Atalanta, tucking the three golden apples into his tunic before the race began. After the start Melanion managed to run decently but then Atalanta picked up the pace. He took one golden apple and threw it to the side. Atalanta could not resist the glimmer the apple gave off so she ran to the side and scooped it up. Melanion kept a very good distance, and again Atalanta began to catch up to him. He threw another golden apple, and Atalanta could not resist it. She detoured and was now carrying a golden apple in each hand.

The finish line was in sight and Atalanta was determined not to lose. With an apple in each hand, she charged towards the end. Melanion threw the final apple behind him and unfortunately, the golden apple landed square in Atalanta's face. She dropped all the golden apples. By the time she managed to gather them all in her arms, Melanion had crossed the finish line. By terms of her contest, she agreed to marry Melanion. But she protested secretly; she never thought someone would win. Knowing Atalanta may resist the ceremony, the King decided she would be married the next day.

150

Atalanta prayed every hour up to the wedding, hoping for some intercession to get her out of the marriage. But alas, Atalanta determined the rules of the contest and many died because of her stakes. No god was willing to answer her prayer.

The moment Atalanta and Melanion were married, Atalanta ran to her garden and sat despondently. She called upon Artemis, her mentor for assistance. Artemis was formal to her, telling her that as a married woman, she would no longer to be a virgin and must leave the wood and the hunt. Atalanta begged for her to never leave as she loved Artemis as she could no other man.

Artemis, in her mercy, said Atalanta could not return to the woods a married woman, but there was another way. She return her to the woods in a way that no one would harm her. Atalanta said that she trusted Artemis, whereupon the goddess transformed Atalanta into a lioness. By virtue of the magic used to bind Atalanta to her, Melanion likewise transformed into a lion. Atalanta, free from the bonds of being a married woman, was free to hunt as she pleased for the rest of her life in the woods.

Narcissus and Echo

Narcissus was a simple boy from a poor family blessed with incredibly good looks and the bearing of a noble prince. His long hours on the farm gave him 4 a defined physique and deep tan many people admired. He was out in the sun with only a modest amount of clothing, so his skin was sun-kissed. But his family was so poor they did not own mirrors. Narcissus had no idea what he looked like.

Many people swooned over him but Narcissus never really noticed them. He was often too busy working to pay attention to the people staring at him with interest. Not only the people but other creatures of the forest and rivers also took time to gaze upon him. Of all of these, the most beautiful of them was Echo, a nymph of the river next to the sea.

Echo was used to seeing herself in reflections of water and admiring

150

herself. She often complimented herself on how beautiful she looked. Then one day by chance, she had to say something out loud that should have been kept to her thoughts: "Even Hera, Queen of Olympus, could not have looked as good as I do today."

Hera's jealousy and vanity is never to be underestimated. For Echo's insult, Hera cursed Echo with "May you always have the last word. But may you never speak first." From that point on, Echo was never able to hold conversations at all. She would only repeat the last thing said. It would embarrass her and the other nymphs ridiculed her. She ran away into a nearby cave to hide in shame.

But Echo could not stay in the cave forever. She would occasionally go to the river look at herself and mourn her loss of her voice. One day, she came across a very handsome man - Narcissus. He was carrying a very heavy load when he saw the river and decided to shed his clothes to bathe himself clean. Echo caught herself staring at him more than her own reflection. She did not believe such a beautiful man could exist.

As Narcissus bathed in the river he looked down and saw someone he had never seen before. He saw someone with a well-defined body and a handsome face. Narcissus was staring at his reflection, but he did not realize it was himself.

Echo, knowing what had happened to her for being so vain, tried to warn him from the same mistake. But she could not speak. Instead, she splashed water to get his attention. but Narcissus still remained staring into the reflection, entranced by himself.

Narcissus spoke to his reflection. "Who are you?"

Echo repeated the word, "You," as part of her curse.

Narcissus thought the person in his reflection was speaking to him. "Me?"

"Me," said Echo.

Narcissus reached out to touch himself in the reflection and saw his hand touch his. He saw his eyes meet himself. When his hand caressed his own chest, the reflection would do the same. Narcissus would talk to the reflection and Echo would repeat the last words of the conversation. Echo could see the handsome man obsessing with the person in the reflection and was too horrified to turn away and too curious to interfere.

Then Narcissus said, "I love you."

And Narcissus believed the reflection said "I love you" back.

Narcissus dove into the reflection for a passionate embrace. He believed he was kissing a beautiful man, a kiss so strong that there was no air. Narcissus promptly drowned in the middle of his kiss.

Echo cried and mourned the loss of this handsome man she did not know. She prayed to anyone that he would not suffer the same way for his vanity. And of all the people to respond to her prayer, it was Hera that answered it, the same goddess who cursed her.

Hera turned Narcissus into a beautiful flower. When several nymphs were searching for Narcissus, they came across Echo who was there in mourning and disbelief that he had been turned into a flower in response to her prayers.

They had also forgotten about Echo's curse. They looked at the beautiful flower first and asked Echo, "Where is Narcissus?"

Echo tried to explain about the drowning man turned into a flower and all she was able to say was "Narcissus."

The nymphs looked around and found his clothes next to the river. They cried over the missing handsome man. All they knew was that the flowers they found next to the clothes he shed were beautiful and they should attribute those flowers to him.

Echo returned to the cave to live the rest of her days.

150

Orpheus and Eurydice

Orpheus was a legend in his own time. Son of the god, Apollo, he played the lyre so beautifully, it left an impression on anyone who heard it. But it also bears noting that Orpheus performed in places where wine flowed freely and medicines that inspired mortals to see visions were heavily abused. So it is not uncommon to hear from his listeners that even rocks and oak trees moved to his music because when you have that many hallucinogens in you, they do.

During one concert, he played next to a river at night and a river nymph named Eurydice came out to dance. As he played, he saw the blue woman dance in the distance. Orpheus did not realize that he was walking towards her as he played the lyre. Eurydice danced as if she were from another world. And when he stopped playing, she finally cast her eyes on him and they fell in love.

When it came time to be married, they asked Hymen, a god who is a guarantor of marriages, to perform the ceremony. They decided that they wanted this wedding to be at night under the full moon with light torches around the wedding site. But they also wanted wine and hallucinogens to be part of the ritual. They sealed the vow with the smoking of herbs and a kiss for ten lifetimes.

As they walked down the path as a newly married couple, in the dark, the roots growing out of one of the oak trees looked like it was moving. She feared that they were snakes. Eurydice began running in panic and Orpheus ran after her. In the midst of running, she fell and tripped over one of the roots of the oak tree. She died when her neck snapped as she landed.

Just as bizarrely, Orpheus in his drug-induced state, snapped the strings of his lyre. When he woke up the next day, he woke up in a pool of his own vomit, next to his dead wife and Hymen offering an herbal drink to clean himself of his poisons. Orpheus did not know what to do. Hymen induced himself with medicine to make himself a channel for all gods and delivered a message. Hymen told him the exact location of the entrance to the Underworld and instructed him to be received by Hades and Persephone to plead for the life of Eurydice.

Orpheus thought this was a sensible plan as any.

Orpheus fixed new strings upon his lyre and brought Eurydice's body next to the entrance to the Underworld. He took a deep breath and entered.

First, Orpheus met Charon. Charon asked for fare to be taken across the River Styx, the entrance to the Underworld. Orpheus began playing his lyre beautifully and sweetly. At the end of his song, Charon had brought him to the Underworld without even knowing that he rowed across the river.

Then Orpheus met Cerberus, the three-headed guardian hound. Orpheus began playing for the three-headed dog and the music lulled the hound to sleep.

Finally he came to Hades and Persephone seated at their thrones. Hades asked what brought him here and Orpheus replied that he came to reclaim his wife.

"Such impudence!" Hades yelled at Orpheus. "I cannot let you reclaim a

150

soul just because you asked! How could you think to do this?" Orpheus was stunned to silence. He did not expect this answer at all.

Persephone looked at the lyre in Orpheus's hands. "What is that?" asked Persephone. "I've never seen something like that before."

"It is a lyre, granted to me by my father, Apollo," said Orpheus. "It sounds like this..." And Orpheus began to play. He played as if pleading. They were more than notes - emotions were plucked from each string. When he was done, Persephone had shed tears and a ghost of Eurydice had been dancing to his lyre. Even when he stopped playing, the ghost continued to dance.

"This must be Eurydice," said Hades and Orpheus nodded. "My queen was very moved and as you know, I would do anything for her, like you would do anything for your wife. So I will make this exception only once..."

At those words, Eurydice stopped dancing and gazed upon Orpheus's face. Orpheus cried in happiness.

"BUT young man, as she follows you out of the Underworld, you cannot look back to see her. You must wait until you completely leave the Underworld before you turn around."

"Why is that?" asked Orpheus.

"Because she is a ghost," said Hades. "She will only follow you in the direction that you look. If you look back, she will assume that she is meant to come back here. And if she comes back, you cannot reclaim her again."

Orpheus bowed in appreciation and headed home. The journey on his way back to the world seemed much longer. As he walked, he could hear none of her footsteps nor her voice. The longer he walked, the more he doubted that she was behind. Passing the sleeping Cerberus, Orpheus wondered if Cerberus would wake up for her. Getting back on Charon's ferry, as Orpheus played, he wondered if Eurydice's ghost had a weight that affected Charon's strokes and if he was rowing for three.

Orpheus arrived at the other side and neared the entrance. Nearing the entrance, Orpheus fell on a rock and tripped, landing hard on his knees. Behind him, he heard a gasp and Orpheus quickly turned around. There stood Eurydice, surprised and concerned. But as Orpheus looked back, Eurydice began walking back towards the Underworld and disappeared.

Orpheus ran to the body of Eurydice just outside the cavern, hoping that what he saw was an illusion, but her body was just as breathless as it had been. Orpheus looked to the cavern but the cavern entrance disappeared, giving him no more chances to reclaim his wife.

CHARON AND HIS THREE HEADED DOG

There was a time when Charon, the ferryman for the Underworld, had gone missing. Without Charon, all the lost souls waited endlessly at the entrance of the Underworld. If we did not find him soon, that line would go out the entrance to the Underworld and the dead would be among the living and ruin the balance of the Universe. I would never have known about this if Persephone had not heard the cries of the three-headed Guardian deep within the lands of the dead.

Persephone led the way, navigating through the shortcuts in the Underworld to get to the entrance where Cerberus was guarding the gate. I found Cerberus taking a nap with his three heads satisfied, lying next to the bones of a slaughtered cow. I resisted petting him but I did squat down to be on his level.

Persephone tugged on the shoulder of my tunic. "Big brother?" she asked in a quiet voice. "I know that you can see into people's heads sometimes so maybe Cerberus knows where he is. Can you do that now?"

"It's a good idea but I can't," I whispered back. It was silly because we were right in front of Cerberus as if he couldn't hear us. "Animals can be read for simple things like anger, fear, and hunger. But complex questions do not work."

"Are you saying he's dumb?" said Persephone out loud. I turned to Cerberus and all three of heads were growling at me. Cerberus was out of his food coma, very awake, and slightly angry.

"No!" I said defensively. "I just don't know if it works!"

"Then why don't you just try it?"

She had a point. I reached out my hand and let Cerberus sniff my hand. The middle head started licking my hand at first, then the other heads were licking it. I got the three headed-dog to calm down.

I sensed through the middle head to see what I could of Cerberus' memories and traces of Charon. But in Cerberus's head, Charon not only had skin, but he was a younger and handsome man. I did not know how I knew it was Charon. I just knew that Cerberus held Charon with so much affection.

They were out in the field. I got the distinct impressions of Charon as a young man saying, "Come on, boy! Let's go!" The field was endless and yet they seemed to be at the edge of the Universe. Those were Cerberus's happy memories and importantly, Cerberus had three heads at the time. I think it meant that Cerberus always had three heads, despite rumors that they were a curse or he was a failed experiment.

I got another image. Cerberus was sad and lonely, wandering by himself. Around him everything was very black. Not dark, but black. I could not even see buildings or trees or mountains. That entire place looked black with no details. Charon was walking by himself when he happened upon a sad, young dog with three heads. Charon knelt down, smiled, and patted him on the center head

"You lost, too, boy?" said Charon. "Come on, we'll go find us a home."

150

Charon acted as if they were already friends.

"Where is this place?" Charon asked as he was walking in the black places. "Cerberus," said the dog with three heads. Charon flinched for a second, not accustomed to talking dogs. "What is your name?" asked Charon. The dog with the three heads made a collective whimper because he did not know. "Hmmmm... until I can think of a name, I will call you 'Dog from Cerberus.'" Charon never did find another name for the dog from Cerberus.

They traveled together, place to place, looking for somewhere they could call home. They went to the ice mountains and Cerberus was too cold. They went to the jungles but the dog found this place so humid and so hot. They went into large kingdoms but Charon felt too stifled. They went into smaller villages and Cerberus was not welcome. They wandered all through the Universe until they settled in some caves. They stayed there for a while. For a very long while, there was chaos outside from war. But the war soon stopped and even then, they had no reason to go outside.

A young man who was pale and boyish of face named Hades came to meet them and asked if they could help. He was just allocated this new place called the Underworld, he said he couldn't do it alone and they looked like they belong there. Charon and Cerberus thought about it and did not mind. Charon only requested that some of the time, he wanted time for himself. Hades welcomed them both. Charon made a kennel for the dog from Cerberus. He even had a plank of wood with the name Cerberus and the name stuck.

Charon ferried the dead across the River Styx. Most of the dead were passive, but some of the dead had died gruesomely. Such exposure to the dead all the time would take a toll on anyone. Even though Charon looked relatively young most of his life and during his travels, he grew old fairly quickly. The dead that died so angrily would tear at Charon, lamenting and saying that their death was not deserved. But he was only there to ferry them, not to make judgments upon them. Yet they would lash out on them, cursing him and infecting him with vileness and diseases, all of which he caught but could not cure. Cerberus took care of those who cursed Charon by devouring them with his three heads.

Eventually, Charon became a living pile of bones and continued to do his job dutifully. And when he was on break, he would always take Cerberus somewhere interesting and new. When they left the Underworld, they looked like what they were when they first met: A handsome young man with wanderlust and a mid-size dog with three heads.

Recently, Charon did not come back. Cerberus waited and waited loyally as he could. But it felt like an eternity for Cerberus. At some point, Cerberus began to howl. Persephone heard the howling all the way in her Court of the Underworld. When she asked what was wrong, Cerberus was in tears. He wanted his Charon back.

I came out of the vision. Before me, all of Cerberus's head were lying down asleep and he was whimpering. Persephone was stroking each of his heads.

"He looks ill," worried Persephone.

"More than ill," I corrected her. "Heartbroken." There was nothing more I could do except find Charon. When he was found, someone had trapped him inside a golden statue in the attempt to keep the dead from traveling to the Underworld, forcing the dead to remain on Earth, disturbing the natural order of things.

When Charon returned, Cerberus was very happy to have his best companion back. There was never a happier howling in the Underworld.

How Charon returned… is a story I will explain later. I promise.

150

POSEIDON VS. ATHENE

Normally, gods only intervened when there was something at stake for them. So when a ruler decided to name his city after a patron god, nearly every god in Olympus wanted that honor.

The king consulted the priests of several temples and they said the destiny of his city could only be secured if a god were to become its patron. Of the many gods who wished to sponsor the city, two of them were among the most powerful: Poseidon, god of the sea and Athene, who was wise beyond compare.

Poseidon went first and struck a rock formation and a river came forth. Poseidon pledged if he were the patron, the city would have a mighty navy and everywhere they sailed, they would conquer. Such a promise was a huge one and many of the men sided with Posideon.

Then Athene came forth. Without much of a spectacular show, she took an olive tree and planted it in the middle of the city. While Posideon laughed, mocking

Athene, she said the olive tree is resourceful. The tree is a hardy tree and can grow in many places. The olives themselves can be food or made into oil. The leaves and the branches also have many uses and this single tree can make everyone prosper. The potential was a huge one and many of the women sided with Athene.

They were both wonderful gifts and the king could not simply decide. However, the queen knew the best decision and she asked her servants to comply. The queen said to the king that until a decision was made, she and her servants would make no food for him.

Over the next couple of days, the hunger got to the king and in desperation, he drank from the river Poseidon made. But the king vomited the water because it was too salty. Feeling sick from the salty river, he went to the olive tree, grabbed a few olives and devoured them, finally satiating his hunger. From this, he made the announcement to the people that Athene would become the patron goddess of the city, and they named it Athens after her.

Poseidon became furious. Gods cannot take back their gifts, but they can "enhance" them as needed. So he enhanced the river he created to flood the newly blessed city. But with Athene's new blessing of protection, Athene told the priests of the city to build boats and they were able to save themselves with no life lost.

Over time, Poseidon's upset feelings with Athens would grow because of his hurt pride. A few generations later when the King of Crete, Minos, came to the throne, Poseidon took advantage of his hubris. He appeared to the king in his dreams and told him it was his destiny to conquer the known the world. If Minos were to dominate Athens first, it would prove to the world what a powerful ruler he is and all others would fall to him quickly. Minos could not forget this dream.

In a matter of a few months, he built a large navy and when the time came, he set sail towards Athens. Meanwhile in Athens, a large gray fog rolled over the city from the ocean. No one knew from where it had come, but it felt ominous. The priests told the men to hide the women and children but it was too late. Several

150

ships sailed in from Crete. The flagship carried King Minos and he ordered Athens to surrender. Athens, a city-state that survived on trade and culture and not on war knew it had not the right protection; so much had gone into learning and culture that there was barely enough military. The sun had not set once and they agreed to surrender. Minos saw there was so much to gain from keeping Athens rather than crushing it so the surrender was a bloodless one, leaving the Cretan navy unblemished with war.

This surrender did not quench Poseidon's revenge. How dare Minos think for himself instead of complying with his plans.

When Minos returned to his home of Crete, an oracle of Delphi gave a message to the king. The oracle claimed Poseidon himself would send him a spectacular bull from the ocean and Minos would need to sacrifice the bull to ensure Athens remained under his control. Minos anticipated the bull coming from the ocean but when it arrived, the bull was ten times the size of a normal bull and just as strong. He ordered a few soldiers to charge into the bull and they were quickly impaled on its horns. Seeing that the task was impossible, Minos convinced himself the oracle's message was somehow misinterpreted. Yet the bull itself did not provoke any attack and seemed to be peaceful. The bull would only attack when it defended itself. The sacrifice was never made and Poseidon was displeased.

Poseidon decided if the bull was too loved to be killed, then so be it. In a perverse revenge, he called upon Aphrodite to lay a charm spell on Minos' wife, Pasiphae, to fall in love with the bull. After struggling for some time, Pasiphae could not deny her passion for the bull and soon became pregnant from him yet Minos was convinced the child was his. When Pasiphae gave birth, she gave birth to a half-man, half bull. He was named "Minotaur" for Minos believed the child was truly his and the half bull part was a blessing from the gods.

Poseidon could not believe the idiocy of Minos, but at least it meant the king would be more susceptible to whatever he had to say.

Over time, Minotaur grew into a very strong creature, stronger than anyone on the island of Crete. And whoever he bested, he would tear apart and devour. The people grew in fear of Minos and Minos did not mind the "respect" they paid to him. However over time, Minotaur was killing some of his father's best soldiers, weakening King Minos' army.

Minos hired one of the best architects in the Aegean Sea, Daedalus, to create a structure that would house Minotaur, leaving him free to wander and yet still be imprisoned. Over a week, Daedalus came up with various ideas until he devised a labyrinth to house the Minotaur. The construction took several years, but when it was completed, it was the greatest structure he had ever created. People wandered in but could never find their way out. To ensure no one would solve the puzzle of the labyrinth, Minos kidnapped Daedalus and his son, Icarus, in their sleep and put them in the middle of the labyrinth.

Although Daedalus and Icarus awoke in the labyrinth not knowing exactly where they were, Daedalus did not panic. He just needed to devise wings for him and his son. For three days, Daedalus and Icarus gathered every feather lying on the ground and every piece of dung. They constructed two sets of wings and Daedalus warned Icarus not to fly too close to the sun for the wings would melt.. Then they launched themselves towards the sky to freedom.

As they flew, they escaped the labyrinth and now they were flying above the sea, looking for a safe place to land. Icarus flew closer to the sun began to fly higher and higher to avoid the dangerous sea below. Daedalus warned him not to go too high but Icarus was too far to hear. Eventually the dung within the wings hardened and began to crumble. Icarus fell towards the sea and was very unfortunate to fall head first on a lone rock above the sea's surface. Icarus died instantly and Daedalus forced himself to be composed until he reached the safety of shore.

Despite Minos' conquest of Athens, he allowed the Athenians to govern themselves as long as they never kept a military and tithed to Crete. The House of Minos continued to watch over Athens but in the meantime, Poseidon's hatred for Athens did not go away. Once the labyrinth was built, Poseidon appeared to Minos
150

again, telling him that too much time had passed in comfort and the youth of Athens are ready to rebel.

Minos had to do something about this, and Poseidon advised him "Remember your son, and what divine signs he must bring." Poseidon put the ideas in Minos' head and Minos decided to leave for Athens right away.

King Minos issued an order to Athens to send their seven strongest sons and seven strongest daughters to the labyrinth as a sacrifice to the divine Minotaur. Should they fail to comply, Minos threatened to raze Athens to the ground. This is exactly what Poseidon wanted. But when the royal House of Athens agreed, Poseidon felt somewhat unsatisfied; he had not expected this answer.

Within the bloodline of the royal House of Athens, there was a prince named Theseus who, despite having only mortal parents was nevertheless blessed with a godlike strength. The rightful king and queen of Athens were forced to live as farmers when their city was taken from them. When Theseus was an infant, his father placed a sword that could cut through anything and a pair of sandals that would carry him long distances under a great boulder. Theseus' mother told her son that when he was strong enough to move the boulder, he was ready to be a man and should take these items to go seek his fortune. If he could move the boulder, for sure he would strong enough to reclaim the city. At age sixteen, he managed to do this so with sword in hand and sandals on his feet, he marched to Athens.

When he arrived, Athens was under the rule of King Minos leaving Theseus with no claim to a throne, but to a protectorate-regency. When Theseus found out about the sacrifices that Minos forced Athens to make, Theseus insisted to be one of the fourteen youth sent for sacrifice. Theseus said that this would prove that he is worthy for the throne of Athens.

Theseus boarded the boat sailing to Crete and upon arrival, the daughter of Minos, Ariadne, fell in love with him and wished for Theseus win. Ariadne, unlike Minos, was fully aware that Minotaur feasts on manflesh is therefore a monster, no matter how much her father was convinced otherwise. Ariadne sought the help of

Daedalus and found him searching for the body of his son to give him a burial so that he may go into the afterlife.

Daedalus gave her a large ball of twine, and said to nail one end of the twine at the entrance and unravel the twine as one traveled further into the labyrinth. To return, the adventurer simply follows the twine back. Daedalus also warned Ariadne that this presented the danger of Minotaur finding his way out, too. She must believe Theseus would be strong enough to handle the Minotaur. As soon as he spoke those words, the body of his son, Icarus, washed on shore.

Before Theseus entered the labyrinth, armed with his sword, Ariadne gave him a kiss for good luck and put the ball of twine in his hands. She instructed him as Daedalus told her. Instead of nailing the twine into the ground, Ariadne decided to hold one end of the twine as Theseus unraveled his end. When Theseus asked why she would do such a thing, she said, "This way, when you win and you wind up the string, you return to me. And if you manage to meet Minotaur and lose, he will follow the string and destroy me. This way my father, the king, will never know who did this." Theseus promised to return to her.

Theseus unraveled the string as planned and at the very end of the string, Theseus discovered Minotaur, feasting on an unlucky sacrifice. Theseus struck Minotaur with his sword while his back was turned and could not even draw blood. The sword strikes were little more than ineffective glancing blows. With the sword and shield useless, Theseus wrestled Minotaur to the ground, squeezing him with his limbs until Minotaur suffocated between his thighs.

Theseus followed the twine back to Ariadne and promptly took her home to Athens, where they were married. Ariadne then returned to Crete with her new husband and presented themselves to Minos.

Theseus revealed himself to be heir to the throne of Athens and the destroyer of Minotaur. Minos, completely enraged at the news his divine progeny

150

was killed, attacked Theseus. But in defense, the prince pulled out his sword to protect himself and his wife. Minos ended up impaling himself on the sword of his son-in-law.

With the marriage of Theseus and Ariadne, the royal houses of Athens and Crete were united. When Theseus eventually became the king, Athens no longer answered to the subjugation of Crete. Likewise, Athene told Poseidon to stop his revenge: To hurt Athens is now to hurt Crete.

Poseidon accepted reluctantly the logic of this reluctantly. He conveniently forgot during the Trojan War. Despite all reasoning, Poseidon can hold grudges indefinitely... Almost indefinitely.

ARACHNE, THE BEST WEAVER ON EARTH

In the stories I have heard about Arachne, it was suggested that Athene could not stand that some mortal woman was a better weaver than her. The Athene I know would not really care that someone has more talent; it is what Arachne managed to do with those weavings that incensed Athene.

Arachne was simple girl in a small village with a single talent: the ability to weave beautiful pictures that told moving stories better than anyone beyond seven mountains away. When she wove a tapestry showing water, the water moved. If you touched those waves, they would ripple and you would swear that your fingers were wet. If she wove ants, if you shook the weaving, you would swear they marched from one end of the weaving to the other.

Arachne was asked by the village elder to weave a tapestry of Athene overlooking the village. It took her one day, one night, one day and one night for her to produce a tapestry. And when the tapestry moved in the wind, it looked as if Athene was walking about the village. The people were overjoyed and praised the weaving of Athene as if she were right before them.

The village would bring parts of the harvest to the weaving of the Athene. They would offer this every day to the tapestry and in the wind, the picture of Athene would say "Thank you" and they would feel blessed. But as time went on, the actual temple of Athene, many walks away, received no tithes and no visitors they the village felt she was there before them in Arachne's weaving.

One day, the goddess herself visited her temple and saw only the servants sweeping. The abandoned temple was twice was clean as any other, but there were no visitors. Athene, in anger, struck her priestesses blind for making no attempt to reach out to the people (matching their lack of vision with actual blindness), balking that they were no better than house slaves.

In the distance, Athene beheld a bustling, busy village with signs of many others traveling there.-In order to relax, Athene went to the village in the guise of an elder woman. In the center of the village stood Arachne's tapestry, being offered fruits, grains, milk and the leftover parts of oxen. Athene could see villagers lined up to present their offerings, and even heard words whispered to them for their sacrifices...

Athene could not believe the mockery the village had made of her. How did they not see the village elder hidden behind the tapestry, speaking for the goddess? Athene, in the guise of the old woman, ranted that the tapestry was not the goddess, it is only but a craft. She attempted to destroy it, but many of the villagers stood in her way. When two of the villagers grabbed her shoulders, her guise disappeared and there Athene stood where all could behold her. Not in full glory, for that would destroy mere mortals, but with enough presence so that all who saw would know she was divine. And fear her.

"Who made this mockery of me?" demanded Athene, whose delicate voice thundered. As Athene walked to the tapestry, a simple girl stood in her way.

"Are you dumb, child?" said Athene, looking at her sternly.

"You will not ruin my weaving!" said Arachne. At this moment, the entirety of the village gasped. Arachne, simple as she was, did not know who stood before her, despite that she had woven her image on the tapestry.

"Do you wish to challenge me?" asked Athene.

"No," said Arachne, "for I do not wish for you to lose…" Arachne did not know the audacity of that statement and this angered the goddess even more.

"I will not lose, child. In fact, for your boldness, I will make you an offer. Should I win, I would like for you to serve me as a priestess for your talent would serve me well. Should you win, you will be a weaver known throughout the world." Arachne consented.

The next day, they began the contest. The judges asked them to weave a picture of the gods in Olympus. Athene wove a picture of the gods in Olympus, feasting on nectar and ambrosia. People felt privileged to see this and marveled at Athene's work. Arachne wove a picture of the gods of Olympus, too. Zeus struck someone with lightning. Poseidon drowned a sailor. Athene and Ares were declaring war on each other using soldiers as pawns. The judges could not decide so they wanted a second day for the contest.

The next day, the judges asked them to weave a picture of love between a god and a maiden. Athene wove a picture of a young Zeus proposing to a Hera (despite that nothing like that had ever taken place…)As people oohed and aahed over Athene's picture, most of the village remarked at Arachne's weaving of Hades kidnapping Persephone from the fields. They knew of this story more than Athene's story. Still, the judges could not decide on the winner, so one more day was decided.

The third day, the judges wanted the contestants to weave a picture of their opponent. This time, Arachne completed her picture of Athene first. Arachne wove

150

a picture of Athene seated regally on a throne. But when the weaving shook, this time, the picture did not seem to move at all. When Athene finished weaving her picture of Arachne, she revealed a picture of a small hideous creature with eight legs. The judges were puzzled by Athene's weaving, saying that it did not look anything like Arachne. Then the judges declared Arachne, the winner.

Athene stood tall and announced that she would keep her end of the bargain that Arachne would be forever known as a weaver to the whole world. With this, Athene touched Arachne's forehead and transformed her into a spider, looking exactly like Athene's weaving. As Athene left, she destroyed the weaving that Arachne made of Athene's image, turned to the people and proclaimed, "Do not mistake a picture for your god." As she left, many followed her back to her temple.

And to this today, Arachne and her kind are the most famous weavers in the world.

Gᴀɴʏᴍᴇᴅᴇ, ᴛʜᴇ ʙᴇᴀʀᴇʀ ᴏғ Zᴇᴜs' ᴄᴜᴘ

Troy is known for many things, especially the folly of its people when they accepted the Trojan Horse. They are also known to have beautiful princes, often instructed to be shepherds. Although such work is often considered beneath royalty, but the logic in making a prince as a shepherd was impeccable:. If a prince could not manage sheep, he will be certain to fail as a king who cannot manage people. So it is no surprise that Paris, who was considered responsible for starting the Trojan War, was found tending sheep when the goddesses Hera, Athene and Aphrodite asked him to decide who was the fairest.

But there was another Trojan prince who tended sheep long before Paris and his name was Ganymede. He was far more learned than Paris and even taught the to sheep herd themselves, leaving him with a lot of free time to sleep or swim in

150

the rivers. One day, Ganymede was bathing in the waters of the Mediterranean when up in Olympus, the eye of Zeus wandered. Zeus caught his glistening body in the water and desire overcame him. Zeus transformed into a golden eagle and swooped towards Ganymede. Ganymede was completely unaware that the eagle was charging and before he knew it, Zeus's eagle talons were carrying the naked body of Ganymede to Olympus.

Zeus kept Ganymede in a room with neither windows nor doors. Ganymede knew nothing about the pleasures of the flesh, which only made Zeus thrilled to teach him those intimate ways. For a long while Zeus had Ganymede as his personal pleasure slave and he did not pursue any other lovers. On top of this, Ganymede was male, so he could never become pregnant.

Because Zeus was not pursuing any other lovers, Hera suspected something was wrong.

Ganymede spent many hours alone in his room, contemplating escape. However, Zeus did provide anything that Ganymede wanted. If he wanted a toy or a game, he got it. If he wanted flowers, even ones that were not in bloom, he got that too. If he wanted clothes that were made of gold, those were given to him as quickly as he demanded it.

The next time Zeus came into Ganymede's room for pleasure, Ganymede asked for another gift. He asked for a cup that would keep things open, wherever they were inserted. Zeus complied with the request, thinking that such an object might have interesting uses. After Zeus was finished taking his pleasure from Ganymede, he left through the wall. Ganymede threw the cup where Zeus departed, leaving a doorway open for Ganymede to escape.

As Ganymede left the room, he entered a banquet hall full of nectar, ambrosia and many feasting gods. Ganymede was not certain where he was.

Hera saw Ganymede and presuming he was a wine server (because he was clutching a cup in his hand), asked Ganymede to pour her some wine. Ganymede thought nothing of this and grabbed a pitcher. But then Hera saw the lovely cup in his hand and insisted she have this cup to drink from. Ganymede gave her the cup and after she had a sip, Hera's mouth stayed wide open. She was unable to speak except garbled words.

Zeus entered when he saw Hera's mouth unable to close and caught Ganymede outside of his room. After Athene removed the cup from Hera's mouth by swatting the back of her head, Hera demanded to know who this incompetent wine server was.

Zeus introduced the feasting gods to Ganymede, his "cup bearer."

Ganymede apologized profusely, saying he did not know that the cup was only for Zeus and no one else. Zeus understood the secret meaning of those words... and so did Hera. Hera simply dismissed this and said to never let it happen again. Hera realized she did not need to pursue revenge on Ganymede; he could never get pregnant and therefore was not a threat to her position. And as long as Zeus's attentions were on him, her husband was less likely to pursue other women. It would not stop Zeus, but it would slow him down.

Zeus was so amused by the outcome that he never punished Ganymede for his crafty escape. And one day when Ganymede asked to become an immortal, Zeus granted this as well.

150

SCYLLA AND CHARYBDIS, A ROCK AND A HARD PLACE

There were so many rumors going around about Scylla, including that she had the loosest lips of any woman in all the Mediterranean, and these were not the lips you found above her chin. This made it even stranger to most people that she spurned the advances of Poseidon. Scylla may not have been the brightest girl, and in fact, bring smart had nothing to do with it. Scylla; from what I heard, was far more the predator of men than prey. Because Poseidon wanted Scylla so badly, she could feel the desperation from his salty loins and it repelled her. Eventually, this angered Poseidon to the point of revenge. But he decided not to kill her... instead, he would do much, much worse.

He had given to one of Scylla's lovers a bubbling, and aromatic bathing-potion in a very fancy bottle to be put into the bath. Not sure how, but I imagine it was not too hard. The lover presented the liquid to her and her four other lovers and they decide to have a bath together with this potion in the ocean. When Scylla's lover first presented her with this gift, she was surrounded by four other men who all enjoyed her favors. She was delighted with this present, and insisted they all rush to the ocean and experiment with it.

So Scylla and her five lovers have an orgy in the ocean, dripped in the aromatic syrup of the bubbling potion. After a few minutes, the bubbling potion felt like burning on their skins. There were moans of ecstasy at first, but they soon escalated to screams of outright pain and terror. A mountain grew under them and the six bodies congealed into a single form of flesh, turning green as the sea. The male lovers all died quickly. But as for Scylla, because the Fates were cruel to her, stayed conscious with her dead lovers permanently attached to her body. Their mouths became her mouths, attached to long necks were always ravenous for bodies to devour; the way she had been hungry for bodies lustfully in life.

Meanwhile, Charybdis was a completely different matter. Many people do not know about her because she was not from Olympus. She came to us as a prisoner from a land very far away from here. I'm not sure what crimes she committed, but rumor had it she was so wicked that she had taken to consuming souls... She came from a place that could not destroy her and could not allow her to remain in that realm. She remains in an ocean prison here, unknown to most.

So it was decided that Charybdis would be kept on Earth near Olympus where she would have very little power. It almost did not matter what her real name was since it has been forgotten; we do not use it and she is generally in a state of eternal sleep. On the surface of the ocean, all anyone physically sees is a whirlpool. But on occasion, some people feel a "presence" that they cannot explain and call that presence it "Charybdis" than what she is actually called. Athene decided in her wisdom to put her next to Scylla, so neither of them would be lonely, but they would disgust each other to be next to each other. It seemed to make the most sense.

But one day, there was more commotion than usual with more roaring and quaking from this area. Athene asked me to check this out since I am diplomatic like

150

my mother, Demeter... Sure.

When I arrived, Scylla and Charybdis were waiting impatiently. The mouths and claws on Scylla roared while the whirlpool on the surface over Charybdis seemed to bubble violently. Instead of trying to calm them down at first (because screaming at monsters will just encourage them to scream back), I floated between, crossed my arms and did nothing until they quieted.

It felt like an eternity, but they managed to quiet themselves. The mouths of Scylla stopped shrieking and the whirlpool whirled slowly but no longer bubbled.; Beneath the waves, I saw a dark, figure of a woman who was suspended beneath the center of the whirlpool, only the curves of her hips and breasts gave away her sex. Her body was limp as if she was drowned, although I knew better. Because Scylla cannot make human speech with her mouths and Charybdis was asleep, I had to use telepathy.

When I asked aloud Scylla what was wrong, I got an image in my head of several ships passing her by. When a ship passed her, six of her long reaching claws would snatch six men and bring them struggling and screaming to her gaping mouths. The mouths would gnash the bones of her doomed victims until they break down enough to swallow the pieces. The men would still be alive as they were swallowed but in no more pain when digested.. I was rather dismayed; not only was this gruesome, it was not what I had asked of Scylla.

Then new images appeared in my head. A couple of ships came back from the West passing by Scylla. On one ship, men were grieving and with them were statues of men who had been petrified on the Isle of Gorgons. The Gorgons were so hideous that a single glance turned them into stone. As the ship passed by, Scylla's claws dropped down upon five of the men... and one of the petrified statues. She crunched down on this statue and immediately began choking on it. She had to use her own claws to rip her bleeding mouth open so she could dig out the man of stone and throw it back into the sea.

A second image came: another ship was passing by Scylla. Scylla was so hungry, she snatched the first six figures and inhaled them. They were all petrified statues. I forced a black out of my mental link because I didn't want to know what happened after. I sensed the men of stone were still in her and unable to come out. All I could sense from her was frustration. She did not like being in pain and always hungry. But there was very little I could do about it.

I turned and spoke aloud Charybdis and asked her the same question I had Scylla. I did not get a reply at first. But when I concentrated on the figure beneath the whirlpool, I could sense something.

It was a place that seemed entirely blue. The water was blue, the air was blue. I looked further beyond the blue and saw a woman in fear of her life. Her eyes were wide, her curly hair was sticking to her face with sweat and she was running through halls that kept changing And within her, a dark presence had taken over her body.

The woman collapsed and reawakened with her eyes not right; all those who saw her knew she had lost control of her body. About five to seven women in blue robes and headdresses surrounded her and it looked like lightning crackled out of their fingers. Two of them were crying, saying there was nothing they could do, begging for mercy against another woman who called for death. She was an innocent overtaken by evil; it was no fault of her own... The other "sisters", that is the word I kept getting, also could not bear to destroy her, but the entity itself was too dangerous to be let out. So the dark presence embodied in this woman was sealed within her. When she was taken away from this place and brought int oour realm, she felt very far from home. Like Scylla, she felt like there was no one to listen to her. At the same time, she understood why she could not leave.

I was not sure what to say, but I had to get back to the matter of the great disturbances they were making.

For a moment, I received nothing from her. Then I got images in my head

150

from Charybdis. They were watery depictions of Scylla ingesting the men of stone. The men sailing away were cheering as Scylla writhed in pain. Random comments yelled so loud as if neither monster would understand them. *Thank the gods she snatched the dead ones. Thank the gods our own crew was put to good use. Take that, Scylla, you foul creature.* All the words of victory were eclipsing the pain Scylla was going through. All through the night, Charybdis heard nothing but screaming pain from Scylla. It was the only noise Charybdis could hear.

I stood there not sure what to do. One monster is in pain and the other has to put up with the noise. I said I would talk to the Gorgons and promptly left. I did talk to the Gorgons (mortals turn into stone, but gods do not) but it did not change anything. They are both still prisoners, still monsters and still meant to be feared. It would be inconvenient to do more. Such is Olympian justice.

KING MIDAS AND THE GOLDEN TOUCH

Apollo was in the chariot in the sky when the king of Argos, Midas, prayed for his kingdom to be prosperous. His kingdom was quite poor and his people were starving. His army had flesh skinner than their spears. They were a hopeful people and they trusted in their king. How all could have trusted a king so much when the kingdom was doing so poorly was beyond explanation, but they were a faithful people and he was a faithful king.

Midas' prayers became exceedingly practical, giving of his comfort so his people may prosper instead. He promised Apollo he would sacrifice his horses so unfertile ground would grow crops. Apollo figured Demeter was in charge of the Earth, and his prayers would be answered by her. But those prayers were unanswered.

150

Midas prayed to Apollo that he would sacrifice his army for bounties of fish in the river. Apollo figured the waters were the domain of the river nymphs so he never bothered to answer his prayer because he assumed the nymphs would hear Midas.

But the nymphs did not.

On the third day, King Midas prayed to Apollo and swore he would sacrifice his only daughter to bring trade to the city and here, Apollo listened. Apollo looked upon this woman… and she was not what we call a beauty at all. Still, Apollo could make her beautiful… it would just take more than a day and one would have to be full of wine and look at her from a distance. In a dream to Midas, Apollo appeared golden and said riches would come to all that he touched, as long as he sacrificed his only daughter to Apollo at the cliff at the end of his kingdom.

Midas awoke. He began touching his bed. He began touching his eating utensils and he began touching the flowers in his garden. To his disappointment, none of them had turned gold as Apollo had promised. But then Midas remembered he must sacrifice his only daughter for such to be true.

Midas told his daughter, Adel, he had a vision from the mighty god, Apollo. He told her a story about a golden flower growing on the cliff at the edge of his kingdom, and insisted only a virgin of royal blood was worthy to pick it and bring it back to Apollo's temple. For this, the kingdom will prosper and he asked his dutiful daughter to do this for him, even though this was an utter lie. And she agreed.

Adel went to the cliff at the end of his kingdom and Midas sent a guard to push her off the cliff without telling her of his plans. When they arrived at the cliff, the guard had a change of heart about performing the terrible deed. The guard warned her of his objective and despite his caution, Adel did not believe him. When she gave up finding the flower, he brought her back to Midas. Midas was angry because the guard did not cooperate and locked him in prison for treason. Midas asked if any of his guards were loyal enough to him to do this task and no one stepped forward. That night, Midas begged Apollo to find someone who was willing to perform this task.

A new man who was recruited the next day, a younger ambitious guard named Milos, decided to do this. He told Midas upfront that this is not for the prosperity of the kingdom but for Milos' own fortune. Midas told Milos he could have anything he wanted in the kingdom. Once Milos agreed, Midas told Adel that Milos would escort her to the cliff to ensure her safety. Even though this was an utter lie. And she agreed.

Milos escorted Adel to the cliff and at each step, and despite that she was not beautiful in the eyes of most people, Milos found himself falling more and more in love with her. When they finally reached the cliff, Milos was completely in love with Adel. Milos confessed her father's plans to Adel, but Adel still did not believe him despite a previous warning. She believed her father too honorable and she continued to search for the golden flower that was not there. She searched from sun up to sun down for this flower that did not exist but still did not believe Milos.

When the sun went away, Milos revealed himself to be Apollo and he took her away into the sky. But when Adel told Apollo of her father's instructions to her, Apollo was appalled Midas had used deceit and cowardice to take advantage of Adel's dutiful and loyal nature. This did not go unnoticed, nor would it go unpunished.

The next day, King Midas awoke wondering of Apollo's promise was kept to him. He touched his bed and it became golden. He touched his dishes and they became golden. He touched the roses and they also became perfect pieces of gold. Midas rejoiced for Apollo's vision had remained true.

People would come to trade with the city of Argos. They would find gold everywhere: flowers, boxes and rings. All of these were gold.

And as they approached the castle, the forms and faces of golden statues displayed intense fear. They were frozen in the middle of screaming, begging and pleading.

Inside the castle, golden statues of naked women were littered about the

150

entrance like vases or potted palms.

In the throne room, Midas sat there, very skinny and gaunt. For any food he touched became gold and useless. And he showed his displeasure by touching the criminals and sentencing them to death by gold.

In Midas' last days, completely hungry and delirious, he offered entire his kingdom for a cure for his ailment. Many physicians came and none could help. In Midas' desperation, he clutched them and they became gold.

Then came a veiled priestess from the Temple of Apollo who stayed her distance and suggested the solution.

"You should cut your own hand off and you will no longer be able to turn things to gold." The veiled priestess tossed him a dagger, which became gold instantly as he touched it. In fury, he cut off his own hand and the blood ran. She tossed him a flower to test if this worked yet that also became gold. She studied this and told him to cut off his other hand. In fury, Midas used the crook of his elbow and determination to cut off his other hand. Midas now had no hands and was crying.

The veiled priestess removed her veil and Adel stood before her father. No longer the young awkward girl he sent to die, she had grown into a stunning beauty. She said, "This is the golden flower I promised to deliver." In agony, Midas said Milos was supposed to have handled her…

"Milos confessed your prayers and became the god, Apollo, before me," said Adel. "He said you would sacrifice me so your kingdom would prosper. Such is the glory of Apollo." Midas, full of pain, said this was not want he wanted.

"But this IS what you wanted," said Adel. "Your kingdom did prosper, just not you. Such is the glory of Apollo."

Adel turned around, heading back to the temple, leaving her father with his wish fulfilled.

Melpomene, the Music of Tragedy

This particular lounge was typical of the many I have been to. There were many chairs for lying around. The lounge was decorated with murals, tapestries, statues and curtains all around the walls. There was someone on one side to serve the wine, mead and juices and a small stage for entertainment on the opposite side. I looked at the list of performers. Sometimes there would be dancers in troupes, live music and sometimes there would be a play. Tonight, there was a singer performing to the soft fire that lit the stage. The singer was Melpomene.

I had heard of Melpomene before. She was one of the Muses; one of the women gifted in the arts. But Melpomene was never known for her singing, but for her tragedy. Tonight, she was not here in any official capacity but to sing her little heart out for the crowd.

Melpomene went on the stage and she commanded a presence. Her dark hair done up in curls, decorated with flowers and pearls and sapphires shaped like butterflies. Her eyes had dark liner to make them stand out from the rest of her olive skin. A dark blue glittering dress clung to her body like the map of the stars in the evening sky; the North Star is where her left nipple is. The light dimmed until it was only around her.

And she began to sing the blues.

Melpomene sang so sweetly, so softly and yet so lovelorn. Always after a performance, there was never a dry eye in the house. The lounge would sell a fortune in handkerchiefs if there were sense enough to sell them. Without one, I wiped my eyes on my own tunic as Melpomene crooned. The stage can only bear her to sing once a week, three times that night, otherwise people would complain about the salt water in the wine.

After her performance, she went down the steps to be among the crowd who thanked her. It was cathartic to cry even when there was nothing to cry about. Because there is always something to cry about, as Melpomene would say.

"Is this seat taken?" she asked when she came to my table.

"Yes it is. It's taken by you."

She smiled at me in half-adoration, took the open seat and touched my hand. "What is my ex doing here?"

"He's listening to you sing. For... cathartic reasons."

"I can sing until you pour your heart out to me," she said with a knowing grin.

"And I think that's why we're not together anymore," I replied, smiling back. She playfully hit my shoulder and laughed.

"Who haven't you been with?"

"Anyone who is a direct blood relation." I emptied the cup in front of me and motioned the serving girl to pour me a refill.

"What are you doing these days? Still working for Athene?"

"Yes, still the same. Meanwhile, you seem to have a new thing going on the side."

Melpomene nodded. "It's been something I wanted to do for a while. One can only write plays for so long until... well... until you find you are better at encouraging others to write plays rather than yourself. Sometimes I find time to sing about that, too. Always the catalyst, never the course. Always the instrument, never the music. Always the fan, never the star."

"Yeah, but not all of us need to be stars. I'm certain it's overrated."

"I'm certain it is. But still, nothing beats the thrill of performing live before an audience, knowing I can fail, but succeed anyway when I hit the high notes. Something like that." The high note she sings comes from such need. It's hard to hold back on a high note.

"Shall I treat you to wine? A songbird has to keep her throat well lubricated."

"True, but I want the vocal control. You should sympathize."

"I do. I'm all about control."

"Yes..." said Melpomene, as if I had said the wrong thing. She moved back her seat and stood up. "If you don't mind, I'm going to be social."

I drank the very last of the wine remaining in the cup. "Melpomene?"

"Yes, Bellaramon?"

"Why did we really break up?"

"I was too much woman for you," she beamed.

"No, really. Why we did we break up?"

Melpomene looked at me for a long while. "If it meant anything to you, you would have remembered." Melpomene bowed her head and departed the table.

150

Tragedy really is an art for her. Because that hurt.

Sisyphus and the rolling Rock

Sisyphus was the King of Corinth who blasted King Zeus for stealing his daughter, Aegina. Normally, even if I knew nothing about the scenario I would tend to assume Sisyphus was right. But this scenario was memorable to me because this time, Zeus did NOT do it.

Keep in mind Sisyphus became king by being paranoid. He schemed meticulously and aggressively against his brothers and sisters coercing them legally to grant him rulership. Sisyphus thought there was no point in killing off his siblings if he could make them work for him. His siblings did so reluctantly, knowing he was capable of inflicting worse states than death to keep his power. Sisyphus believed in his heart he was very similar to King Zeus; keeping his siblings beneath his heel was proof enough of his divinity.

150

One day he saw a large golden eagle carry a maiden in the sky. He looked and believed that he saw his daughter, Aegina, being carried away and immediately thought that the large golden eagle was actually Zeus in disguise. Sisyphus immediately assumed he was witnessing Zeus carry off his favorite daughter.

He stormed to the nearest priest of Zeus and demanded, absurdly even for a king, to he see Zeus right away. The priest tried politely to refer the king to the Oracle in Dodona, but King Sisyphus began to holler and threatened to murder the priest if Zeus did not answer his summons. The priest, scared out of his mind, begged and pleaded in mumbling and sobbing tears that his master, Zeus, come to him.

Zeus arrived displeased.

Sisyphus angrily accused Zeus of kidnapping his daughter but Zeus said he had not done so. The King of Corinth took it a step further and accused Zeus of lying. Zeus took his priest's tears and formed a pool before Sisyphus, showing, Aegina, was safe in her own room.

Yet Sisyphus still did not believe Zeus and cursed some more. Zeus was at the edge of his temper when he tried to be rational and asked how he came to this conclusion. Sisyphus, feeling his own words were not enough, invented a river god by the name of Asopus. According to Sisyphys, Asopus reported seeing Zeus become a golden eagle and snatch his daughter away. Some people may have nerve, but to first accuse Zeus of lying and then telling a lie in turn was beyond Zeus' tolerance.

There was no point in being rational nor wasting his time. Zeus struck Sisyphus with a lightning bolt and killed him.

When Sisphyus' soul reached the Underworld, Zeus was not content to let this arrogant man just wander like everyone else. He carried Sisyphus's soul by the scruff of his neck and threw him at Hades' feet. Zeus was breathing hard, furious when he appeared before brother.

"What exactly did he do?" asked Hades, puzzled by the soul tossed before him and Zeus' anger. At this point, Zeus went into a tirade so angry and quickly spoken, it sounded like a squirrel cackling.

Zeus wanted a torture so horrible that hearing it would strike terror into his enemies. Hades pointed out Sisyphus was annoying and irrational, not evil and unjust. Zeus hated Hades' logic but asked what Hades would do.

Hades brought Sisyphus to the bottom of a hill where sat large boulder and explained his task was simple. If Sisyphus managed to get the boulder to the top of the hill and have it stay there, he would be able to continue through to the rest of the Underworld. Sisyphus pushed the boulder up the hill and felt that it took some effort, but it was possible. However, when Sisyphus got his boulder halfway up the hill, portions of the hill began to collapse under his feet. He lost his footing and the boulder rolled back down the hill.

Zeus examined the hill and saw it was made of very fine sand. Whenever there was too much weight on it, the hill would collapse. Zeus smiled at the idea.

"Brother, at some point the hill will erode and become flat. Would not the task be accomplished then?" asked Zeus.

"It could," said Hades. "However..." Hades led Zeus a very long distance to the other side of the hill. There, Zeus watched some other man digging a hole in the sand towards something at the bottom but that hole seemed to keep filling up by itself with more sand. However, all of the sand that was dug was tossed to a large mound behind him... creating the large hill where Sisyphus kept trying to roll his boulder.

"Brilliant," declared Zeus.

150

PEGASUS AND BELLOPHORON

The gruesome tale behind the birth of Pegasus is that he was born of the blood of the slain Gorgon, Medusa. When Perseus cut of her head, Medusa's body slumped and the boiling blood gave rise to a beautiful white winged horse named Pegasus. But this is not entirely true.

Perception played a very strong part;. Perseus simply thought Pegasus was born a full horse with wings from the blood of the Gorgon. In reality, the winged horse simply saw the slain flesh and smelled blood while it was in the dark skies over the Isle of Gorgons. Perseus failed to notice (being too busy avoiding the Gorgon's stare) that Pegasus simply swooped down and began eating the dead flesh. Perseus had never seen the winged horse until this point so he logically concluded (and this is why I cannot trust humans with logic) Pegasus was born from the blood of a Gorgon.

Pegasus was originally a rejected horse of Helios. Helios originally drove the sun chariot led by fiery horses in the sky to provide the daylight. In order for the horses to handle the heat and fire of the sun, Helios anointed them with magic so they would suffer no burns from their skins blazing with fire. When Helios came to Pegasus, the winged horse refused and bucked his reins until he was free to roam the Universe.

Without having a master to care for him, Pegasus learned to survive his own way. He found sustenance by feasting on the newly dead, no better than a vulture. When there were no newly dead to be found, he would feast on whatever flesh was available, living or dead, making Pegasus a creature of unspeakable terror. Like a siren, he was beautiful and alluring but no one spoke of his beauty for they could not have lived long enough to survive Pegasus' speed or his teeth.

Yet a boy named Bellophoron would not be swayed from taking Pegasus as his horse. While playing in a meadow with his friends, he saw the most beautiful horse drinking from a river. The horse was so beautiful that the enraptured Bellophoron failed to hear the screaming of people, Pegasus' last meal was still alive, portions of his body were eaten. The horse and the boy looked at each other in a long stare before the horse flew away. While Bellophoron's friends ran away when they saw the blood dripping from the horses' mouth, the boy wanted to conquer the unconquerable wild horse.

Bellophoron decided he needed the aid of the gods to do this. Most would have advised the boy against such folly, but it was none other than Athene who came to him in a dream. Athene's logic in helping him was simple: Either this boy dies in the attempt to rein in a very dangerous creature and the world is less one idiot; or he manages to get the horse and removes this menace from the Universe. In either case, the world wins. Athene granted him a magic bridle that would be used to ensnare the Pegasus. Any horse upon seeing the bridle would be charmed by it and any horse wearing the bridle would obey its master. Bellophoron was happy to be blessed by Athene and went on his way to find Pegasus.

The next day, Bellophoron found Pegasus again in the same meadow

150

drinking the same water. He showed the magic bridle to Pegasus and the horse did not seem to move. Bellophoron quickly tacked on the bridle and mounted the horse. Pegasus began to fly wildly until the boy had enough sense within him to tell the horse to stop and land. It worked and the horse was his.

Meanwhile, Bellophoron liked showing off his impressive steed. Since Pegasus now had a master, he was able to eat grain again rather than scavenge for food. Because Bellophoron could now fly through the skies, he accepted messages and was able to deliver them quickly. It was to the point where the other couriers were losing business and some of them were starving. King Proteus of Argos especially did not like this. Argos had already gained a fortune through trade, thanks to King Midas many ages ago, but Bellophoron stopped a particular strategy of trade. Argos normally sent messenger ships to other cities full of unwanted cargo and unloaded cargo at those cities. Because the city was so economically powerful, refusing ships from Argos could destroy a city's trade. With Bellophoron delivering messages, most messenger ships stayed in their docks, and the economy of Argos was growing stagnant.

King Proteus of Argos decided to hire Bellophoron to send a message to the King of Lycia. Bellophoron took great pride in this assignment and went to Lycia with haste. The King of Lycia, Xerandus, bid Bellophoron to stay at his palace while he opened King's Proteus's message.

The message read: Destroy the messenger before you.

King Xerandus did not want to be responsible for killing Bellophoron outright. After all, the boy has a nice horse and the King promised him hospitality. Furthermore, he had nothing to gain by doing this favor for the King of Argos. However, he did have to make some kind of effort.

The next day, King Xerandus, ranted about a horrible creature in the mountains west of Lycia and he could not find a champion willing to destroy it. Bellophoron wanted to know more and Xerandus told him the Chimera was in a mountain pass, barring people from coming or going. Xerandus also said it was a terrible creature with a head of a lion, body of a goat and a tail of a snake. Feeling heroic, Bellophoron said he was up for the challenge and simply asked for a bow and arrows he could light on fire.

Bellophoron rode Pegasus and flew west to the mountains to find the Chimera. When he saw the creature, it was a large creature but the description seemed somewhat inaccurate; Bellophoron encountered a very large lion at first that swiped at him with razor sharp claws. Then the creature shape shifted into a ram with spiky fur and attempted to ram the flying horse. Then the creature shape shifted into a snake with three heads, spitting venom at Bellophoron. The boy rode the horse skillfully, avoiding all the attacks. When the Chimera shape shifted into a lion again, Bellophoron shot a fiery arrow into one of its eyes. As it screamed in pain, the Chimera shifted into a goat, and the boy shot into the other eye. The Chimera shifted for a third time into a snake with three heads and one head darted at him. When the Chimera opened its mouth wide, Bellophoron shot a fiery deep into its bowels and the head caught on fire. The creature burned into a lump of dead flesh and Bellophoron was victorious.

Believing he deserved glory, Bellophoron rode the Pegasus to go higher and higher, believing he could reach Olympus and join the gods. He rode higher and higher and the air became thinner and thinner. Soon the air was so thin that Bellophoron could not breathe. He lost consciousness and fell off Pegasus, who still continued to fly higher into the sky until he reached Olympus. Bellophoron fell to Earth and his body was never found.

Zeus found Pegasus in Olympus and put him into a stable. Zeus made the mistake of removing Athene's magic bridle and Pegasus promptly bit Zeus on the hand. Zeus immediately landed a punch into Pegasus' face as a reaction and the horse knew never to do that again. Pegasus began to crave flesh again. For better or worse, Zeus let Pegasus out once every few days to eat his fill.

150

Phaëthon and the Chariot in the Sky

Phaëthon was a very handsome, golden haired boy with deeply tanned skin and a wiry build. His mother, Clymene, raised him alone and whenever Phaëthon would ask about his father, she quickly changed the subject or gave him food. Regardless of how much food she gave him, he never seemed to gain any weight. This concerned Clymene because she feared there would come a day when there would be not enough food to feed him.

One day, Phaëthon asked about his father again and she promised she would tell him when he was old enough. Phaëthon asked if his father was dead, but she admitted that he was very much alive. He became sad. If the father was alive, did he not want his son? Did his father want nothing to do with him? Is he the reason why his mother raised him all alone?

Many days passed and Phaëthon refused to play out in the sun because he had become more and more depressed, thinking he was not wanted by a father he never knew. His appetite was gone and soon he was eating nothing at all. Now Clymene was concerned he wither away and die.

Unable to keep the secret anymore, she revealed to him that his father was none other than the God of the sun, himself, Apollo, riding the chariot in the sky. When Phaëthon heard the news, he was both excited and perplexed. Excited that his father was a god and perplexed why his mother never wanted to tell him.

"Phaëthon, I suspected you would never have believed me if I told you. That maybe my head was soft or I was full of delusions. No one else believed me when I said this and they only called me a liar. So rather than humiliate you, too, I decided to say nothing until now."

"Mother," said Phaëthon. "It is not impossible for me to believe. I have been told I had a special look about me throughout the village with golden hair and tanned skin as if I were a child of the sun." However, Phaëthon was not as discreet as his mother. The next day, he bragged about his divine parentage and the other boys began to laugh and mock him.

"Oh really?" said one of the boys. "Your father is really Apollo, the Sun god and driver of the fiery chariot?"

"Of course!" said Phaëthon very proudly.

"I bet you do not even know him!" said another of the boys. Although they were right, he could not stand there and accept it. He looked at the sun, where his father was high in the sky, for inspiration. The sun would blind most boys but Phaëthon was determined to not be ridiculed.

"He even let me drive the chariot once!" said Phaëthon. He pointed to the sky. "See? That's one big wheel and on the on the other side... there's... another wheel..." In Phaëthon's head, this sounded good until he spoke. But he felt humiliated and ran home.

Phaëthon cried to his mother, "Why can't I see my Father?" Clymene knew

150

the time had come. She told Phaëthon to go to the closest mountain east of here and climb to the very top before the sun rose. And there he will see his father.

Phaëthon woke up very early while the sky was still dark and climbed the mountain to the east. There he saw a stairway and he climbed it. When he arrived, he saw a shining palace made-of gold. Phaëthon entered the palace and he saw Apollo sitting on the throne, smiling at him.

"Welcome, son. Your mother let me know you were coming." Phaëthon confirmed Apollo was indeed his father and Apollo threw his arms around him and kissed him. "I know I was not there for your life and it was your mother's choice to raise you alone. But I will give you whatever you like. This I swear upon the river Styx."

The oath by the River Styx is a very important one. To most people Styx is simply a river in the Underworld. To the gods, it is not a mere oath. To break such an oath means you are willing to give up your power and your immortality, something the Fates decreed to keep the promises of the powerful vigilant.

Phaëthon knew what he wanted. "I want everyone to know I am actually your son, so I wish to drive the Chariot of the Sun."

The smile on Apollo's face became nervous laughter. "Maybe you should think in grander terms, Phaëthon. I can give you so many riches so that you will want for nothing. I can make you such a brilliant strategist that people would fear you in war. I can make you the best healer in the world, able to cure nything except death." Phaëthon was still insistent on driving the Chariot of the Sun. Apollo asked Phaëthon to hold for a moment.

Apollo walked away and called out to Hermes. Hermes arrived as instantly as Apollo called him.

"Hermes, is there a way to get around the oath of the river Styx?"

"Yes," said Hermes. "Do not swear on something you cannot deliver." Apollo cringed.

"I promised my son, Phaëthon, to give him anything he wanted and he wants to drive the chariot of the Sun. And I know he has never driven a chariot before. ANY chariot."

"Idiot," said Hermes. "Well, you could decide to be mortal."

"No, I would rather Phaëthon drive the Chariot."

"Well, I guess you have your answer." With that, Hermes promptly left.

Apollo forced a smile and led his son to the stables. He made Phaëthon meet all the fiery horses. He made Phaëthon brush their coats, which were very hot but he managed to do them. He made him clean up their dung. He made him feed them and one of them nearly bit off his hand. After all of these tasks, Phaëthon still wanted to drive the chariot.

Apollo went over the instructions at least three times, making sure Phaethon knew how to control his six fiery steeds and how to take a single path from one end of the Earth to the other. He warned his son not to go too high, otherwise the Earth will freeze. He warned Phaethon not to go too low, otherwise the Earth will boil and burn. He finally gave Phaëthon the reins and watched nervously as the boy set out in the chariot.

Phaëthon did not start off too badly. He paid careful attention to Apollo's instructions and watched the Earth. If it looked a bit cold, he would move closer to the Earth. If it got too warm, he urged the steeds to fly higher. So Phaëthon, for someone who has never driven a chariot before, was quite attentive and somewhat impressive.

That was, until Phaëthon saw his friends below. He decided ~~that he~~ to lower himself so they could see him and thereby prove he was indeed the son of Apollo. As he saw his friends and waved to them, the village began to get incredibly hot, especially since he was circling the area instead of journeying one end to the other in an arc. When the boys who mocked him looked up and gasped, Phaëthon wore the widest smile on his face. But then the village burst into flames and the
150

people melted like candle wax.

Phaëthon freaked out and urged the steeds to move. The fiery steeds began to panic and Phaëthon no longer was able to control the chariot.

Several of the gods looked from Olympus and heard all the commotion from Earth. Zeus looked and he did not recognize the chariot driver. Zeus threw a lightning bolt at Phaëthon, whereupon Phaëthon fell from the chariot and died.

At the end of the night, Zeus asked Apollo to explain why he let someone so inexperienced drive the most important chariot in the world. Apollo answered: he swore on the river Styx to get anything his son wanted.

"Idiot," Zeus replied.

ARIADNE AND LIFE AFTER THESEUS

Not all stories have a happy ending. But sometimes, an unhappy ending serves as a new beginning.

Ariadne, Princess of Crete, lost her father when he was impaled by Theseus' sword. Her father attempted to attack Theseus and he simply lifted the sword towards his chest. To lift Ariadne's spirits, Theseus proposed they go off far away together before returning to Athens, so they set sail to Persia. The first night in Persia was magical, heavy with perfume and Ariadne felt she had slumbered for days.

When she awoke, Theseus was gone. Everything about him was gone. When she asked about her husband, only one old woman told her Theseus left, telling others he was leaving a common slave girl behind. Not only was she

150

heartbroken, but she felt completely betrayed. She wept for days and wandered Persia until she arrived at a group of women, feasting on wine and frolicking in ritual, calling themselves Maenads. They looked to be without a care in the world, dancing violently, bodies crashing into each other. Standing among them was the leader, the god Dionysus, god of the vine and festival legend. The bodies around him crashed into him but he did not move.

Ariadne wept and threw herself into the fray of bodies until she could grab hold of Dionysus' blood and wine stained feet. She begged to forget love and life and Athens and Crete in her passionate outcry. Ariadne believed only Dionysus could help.

Dionysis bid Araidne to strip her clothes and walk with him to the river Euphrates. She assumed she was going to lie down with him so she wanted to present herself as seductively as possible. But Dionysus did not pay any attention to this as he guided her to stand among the flowing waters.

"Today, you leave us as Ariadne," said Dionysus and pushed her into the water. She fell with no resistance, for there was nothing to stand for anymore. She stayed below water for a long time and thought her life would expire there. But then as death crept upon her, she wanted to cry out and breathe. With this desire, she reached out her hand and Dionysus' hand touched hers. He pulled her from the water and Ariadne was breathing so hard, she was crying.

"Welcome back, Ariadne. You are now a new woman." She threw her arms around Dionysus and thanked him for her salvation. He asked if she still wished to be called Ariadne and she nodded. Dionysus reached deep into her heart and asked what she wanted to do.

"I want to be yours," said Ariadne. Dionysus grew ivy from the ground and broke it in two. He made one strand of ivy as a crown and put it on her head. He took the other strand of ivy and put it betwixt their hands.

"You are my wife now," said Dionysus. "And you have nothing. You are not a princess and you have no standing and you have had everything taken from you. You are free and always will be. And now nothing will abandon you."

Ariadne lived out the rest of her days in quiet but happy poverty. When she died, Dionysus took her body and placed it among the stars.

Endymion and the Sleep under the Moon

In nights of old before Artemis, the twin sister of Apollo, drove the chariot of the moon, a Titan by the name of Selene drove the Moon chariot, led by six white stags that flew through the sky.

One night, Selene looked down and saw the most beautiful boy, a shepherd named Endymion. The night Selene saw him, he had been searching for his sheep. His task took so much time that, by the time he found his sheep, there was no time to return home. So he decided to sleep on a hillside. Selene wishing to see him again, decided to use magic to make him slumber longer.

The next night she saw him again, she desired to kiss him, touch his hair, smell the musk of his hard work and know what was underneath his tunic. For many days, she dreamt about him to the point of punishing herself. Eventually the thought of him drove her to near madness.

One night, instead of taking the chariot to the sky, she went straight to

Endymion and touched and kissed him in his sleep. He still breathed but had not awoken for many nights. Weeds were growing around him as if the Earth were going to take the beautiful boy into her embrace, but Selene cleared those weeds like a jealous lover. And then she had her way with him without waking him at all.

Selene would do this once a month for several years. Somehow, Endymion would never grow old and would never wake up. No one in the world knew that he was missing although they would occasionally wonder what took him away many years ago. Rumors would say had been snatched up by some goddess, not knowing that they were partly right.

But one night, Selene left her chariot behind to be with the sleeping Endymion. It so happened that Zeus was looking out in the stars and the sky and had no idea where the Moon was. He asked Hermes to search for the Moon. Hermes went to the Palace of the Moon and saw the Moon chariot there with the six white stags still in their stables. Hermes searched far and wide for Selene and finally found her pleasuring herself with the sleeping young man. Hermes started laughing when he found out, loud enough for Selene to be afraid. She looked up and begged Hermes not to tell anyone. But Hermes said, "Zeus, already knows that the Moon is not there."

Selene, in desperation, asked Hermes to tell Zeus the white stags that pull the chariot have been shot with arrows and could not move. Hermes knows this is a lie but he promised her he would relay this to Zeus.

Hermes returned to Zeus and told him the white stags had been shot. Artemis, the Goddess of the Hunt heard and immediately ran over to the Palace of the Moon, to see if she could tend to the stags' wounds. However, when she arrived, she saw those stags were unharmed. Artemis was furious with Hermes for telling such a lie, and Hermes chided Artemis for being so impatient when he was about to explain Selene asked him to say this.

Zeus demanded to know why Selene wanted to relay a lie and Hermes

150

made some subtle gestures suggesting what she was actually doing. Zeus found this hilarious and laughed out loud with Hermes. Artemis, however, was displeased that Selene would tell such a lie.

Artemis found Selene still pleasuring herself with the sleeping Endymion. Artemis decided to take her silver bow and arrow and shoot the back of Selene's thigh. Selene screamed in pain. Selene glared at Artemis for wounding her but Artemis returned a stare just as cold.

"How dare you tell the ruler of Olympus the stags were wounded! Maybe before you tell such a lie, you should know what such a wound feels like!" Before Selene could protest, Artemis continued further. "From now on, I will drive the chariot of the moon in your stead so that you can spend precious time with your boy." Artemis left before Selene could respond.

When Selene looked back at Endymion, he was waking from his sleep. But a few moments later, his breath became unsteady and he expired. With sleeping for so long under magic and no food to sustain him, Endymion's body stopped functioning and decayed. Selene cried and went into fits of anger. While in anger, she went to the Underworld and left the identity of Selene behind. She took up the name, Hecate, knowing all would fear it and threw herself into her magic, spurning all affection and dedicating herself to the craft.

PYGMALION AND GALATEA

Pygmalion was an unsuccessful artist. Although he was able to make sculptures of people, he would play with the proportions so they never seemed quite right. One figure would have ears hanging down to her chin. One figure would have arms down to her knees. One figure would have breasts off to the side and under her armpits. He was given to interpretation, but patrons did not like his art. Without a patron, he could not live life as an artist, so he went into construction where he could at least work with similar materials.

Meanwhile, this man was sexually frustrated. He wanted to be with the women who would prance by the construction sites, but they were pock marked or visibly diseased. These women were prostitutes and they had very short lives. Pygmalion became paranoid of sleeping with them for fear of catching anything. As

150

time went on, he began to pick them apart until he had no interest in the women at all.

Pygmalion was so frustrated that at one point, he took a large piece of marble home and began to sculpt it. His hammer and chisel dug into the marble repeatedly until he formed a woman so lifelike, he had to stand back and marvel what his frustration had done. He had sculpted a faithful recreation of a woman's form, anatomically distinct. In his loneliness, he stripped and laid with the statue, smothering her with kisses and even inserting himself into this statue.

Each night, he fell more and more in love with it. He pretended she was real and told her about his day. He began bringing her flowers and sweets. He brought her clothes and fit them on her. He continued to make love to her each night, ignoring that she was a marble statue that did not kiss or caress back. He even began calling her "Galatea," after an old childhood friend that he had a crush on a long time ago.

One night Pygmalion came from work, very frustrated and sweaty and he ravished Galatea as he never had. She did not bend or move as he released himself into her. She did not react or feel passionate towards him. When Pygmalion was done, he looked at her and began crying. He could no longer ignore that this woman was not really a woman at all.

There was a festival for Aphrodite, and Pygmalion decided to attend. He wrote his wish, to find a woman like Galatea to be his wife, on a piece of paper and threw it into the altar fire. The paper rose as it burned and became ash. Pygmalion had no idea if the goddess, Aphrodite, heard his request.

Aphrodite was in Olympus, gathering pieces of paper burned in the altar to her. Of the many requests made, she picked up one laden with salty tears and read Pygmalion's request. Aphrodite was saddened by how pathetic this was; this man wanted a human woman no better than a statue, without any regards to her wishes or her feelings. But still, she was amused by the idea of what would happen if this woman was real, WITH feelings, desires and thoughts independent of his own.

The goddess visited Pygmalion's house and saw the statue of Galatea. She saw that he brought her dresses, flowers and sweets. The flowers were slightly wilted, obviously picked for her a few days ago. The sweets were not at all touched and Aphrodite was afraid that this was slightly unclean. Aphrodite began looking at the form and realized that the man must be frustrated yet skilled because this woman was anatomically correct and he had been using her for that purpose. Aphrodite figured at least this woman would be well cared for and bringing Galatea to life would harm no family.

Aphrodite awakened Galatea, who was nude and sleeping on the floor.

Pygmalion arrived later that night and went towards Galatea. But the statue was gone. Pygmalion was heartbroken, thinking that the goddess had punished him and taken her away from him. As he cried, a woman with a shift came and put her hands on his shoulders and asked what was wrong. Pygmalion cried and said the good goddess punished him for asking something so ridiculous. The woman asked what he wished for and at this moment, Pygmalion realized that he was actually not alone and turned around. Here was this woman who looked exactly like this statue who was smiling at him, talking to him; and despite that she did not know him at all, she was comforting him.

He smiled nervously and did not know what to say. The woman bade him to get up from the floor and put him to bed. She said he looked like he needed rest. Because there was only one bed, she asked if it was alright that they sleep in the same bed. Pygmalion said this was alright, as nervous as he was. When she came to bed, her skin touched his and his eyes went wide. Her skin was familiar, but this time it was warm.

"Galatea?" asked Pygmalion.

"Yes, what is it?" replied Galatea.

150

Pygmalion turned to her and smiled. He did not use her at all that night, content to have a happy warm body in bed alongside him. Eventually, when they did make love, he fit perfectly into her. After all, he sculpted her and he was THAT skilled.

Aurora and Tithonus

What does the Goddess of the Dawn do, anyway? Apparently, most people think that she's some pretty woman with a beautiful cloak who prances about when the sun rises. Why would Zeus want someone so useless serving him?

Back when the night was too dark and there was no guaranteed moon in the sky, those who lived in the dark prayed for sanctuary. This is what Aurora provided, sanctuary for those who could not fend for themselves in the dark. When the dawn came, people were finally safe. So people began to pray for dawn, a sign of Aurora's sanctuary. But over time, poets and artists only remarked on the colors of the dawn because it was so visually striking. It seems Aurora is so beautiful people forget she is practical and failing to see this is sad.

150

When Aurora married the mortal Tithonus, she asked Zeus to bestow upon him the gift of immortality so that he would be with her always. Zeus agreed, making the new couple very happy. But as time went by, Aurora realized she had forgotten to ask for eternal youth to go along with his immortality. She watched him grow old and frail and as time went on even further, he became senile and babbled when he talked. Aurora was not sure what to do.

I remember this clearly because she was freaking out and looking for Athene, who would know the wisest course to take. She felt terrible for inflicting "gift" this on the man she loved. She did not find Athene; she found me instead. She had been drinking so much kona it was almost impossible to calm her nerves.

I asked if it was possible to just stab him with a weapon; if he was so far gone out of his head, he would not feel pain and it would be out of mercy. She admitted she tried, but because of the gift of immortality, arrows would deflect off of him, swords would bend away and fire would burn him but he would not die. I remarked that her answer was too precise to have been theory.

"If he were an inanimate object that you would have to put away, how would you put it away where you would never have to deal with it?" I asked.

"Throw it in the ocean?" she asked.

I thought of Poseidon and how messy this would be if Tithonus were simply tossed there like a piece of trash. "Hmmm... maybe somewhere where no one ELSE has to deal with it?"

"In the sky?" she suggested.

"That works," I said.

Aurora attempted to set Tithonus among the stars but he kept falling out of the sky. After several tries, she took Tithonus, who was completely out of his mind, and turned him into an insect that we now know as a cricket, an insect that continues to babble in the middle of the night.

Aurora never fell in love nor asked an Olympian for a favor ever again.

Prosymnus and the Male substitute

For all the wild parties that Dionysus throws; everything from tasting the first wines of the season to wild orgies filled with herbal spiked wines (the latter is more popular and more fun), Dionysus himself is not as wild as people thinks he is. In fact, he conducts himself more like a master of ceremonies while everyone else lets loose. And once everyone else has had their fun, he begins to indulge. Despite this, he is still never quite sober. The lack of sobriety can affect one's mind, as well as other body parts.

One of his orgies was held out in the middle of nowhere, where he had grown elaborate structures made of vines. I remember the wine served was especially potent. It was so sickeningly sweet; I could not bear more than a sip, so it did not affect me very much. But it managed to affect even the God of the Vine

150

himself.

I remember distinctly that in this state, he was so drunk that a certain part of his body could not "stand to attention". Unfazed and totally naked, Dionysus pulled out a wooden phallus to satisfy his partners. This distracted me so much that my partner had to force my head back to what I was doing, but I thought that using a wooden substitute was kind of humiliating. (I remember Dionysus trying this on me once. It was not for me.)

I remember at another one of his parties, one where Dionysus was purposely trying to get me drunk, I asked him where he got the idea of using a wooden phallus. "I got it when I went to save my mother's soul from the Underworld to take her here to Olympus," he said. I could not have gotten a more disturbing answer. So here I take Dionysus' own words and put it to page:

"There is a particular way to get into the Underworld, and it was the way most people go: You die to get in. However, there is another way into the Underworld that Hermes told me of. To cause less commotion, I took the route that Hermes mentioned; taking my mother out of the Underworld was not meant to be public news. I especially had to keep the news away from Hera, who would have tried to prevent me from rescuing my mother. Her vengeance is boundless." (Note to readers: Dionysus' mother was the Princess Semele of Ethiopia.)

"This route is at the bottom of the Alcyonian Lake, which mortals think is a bottomless lake. But if you hold your breath long enough, you will sink to the entrance. But I could not take all this time to search for that entrance. There was only one person, who tended the lake's fish and knew this lake well. His name was Prosymnus and he swam so often in that lake, you would think he was a water nymph. Furthermore, that lake is quite dangerous; many swimmers have been known to drown in its still waters.

"When I asked Prosymnus to take me to the center of the lake, being wary to explain exactly why, he charged a simple fare: He wanted to have sex with me. Well, I had to rescue my mother... and he was an attractive enough young man, with dark hair and a body like a firm willow. Of course, I was going to say 'yes.' But I would have to get together with him later AFTER I rescued my mother."

I interrupted here. "Well, obviously it worked. Semele is here in Olympus as a naturalized goddess. Much to Hera's displeasure." Dionysus gave me a sly smile. "But it still does not explain your wooden... male substitute."

"I was getting to this. I left the Underworld the normal way, through the caverns, passing a sleeping Cerebus. Charon did not bother to stop me when I gave him a skin of one of my best wines. So I did not see Prosymnus again at all. But then later, I got word Prosymnus had died. From what I understand, he was swimming in the lake when his body racked in pain suddenly and he fell into the mouth of a large fish. A tomb was erected for him because he did save the lives of so many who would have perished without his assistance.

"...And so, I wanted to keep my promise to Prosymnus. I carved a wooden phallus and affixed it to his tomb and... inserted him into me... until he satisfied me."

I looked at Dionysus long and hard. "I honestly do not know if it is the effect of your wine talking but if I did not see your truthful aura, that sounded like the most ridiculous reason to come up with a wooden phallus."

"Bellaramon, I swear upon the River Styx that this actually happened." With those words, I knew that I could not contest Dionysus' tale.

I thought about this some more and asked, "Why didn't you go back down to the Underworld, find Prosymnus, and have your way with him?"

Dionysus' smile was more cordial now. "Bel, I would go to the torturous Underworld to get my mother back. I would not go to the Underworld just to lay."

150

Oaths by the river Styx

Everyone knows that an oath by the River Styx is the utmost important oath that anyone an immortal can swear. It is unbreakable no matter who swears this. Well, the reality is that it is not "unbreakable," but the consequences are rather dire. To a human, swearing to this river does not really mean anything; it's like breaking a promise that you make yourself. To a god, swearing by the River Styx in the Underworld means that as a god, you are willing to give up all your power and immortality behind to keep this oath. It is a tradition that no one dares break in Olympus and no god is beyond it. And this particular tradition began when Zeus was seizing the power of Olympus from his father, Kronos.

This river in the Underworld was named after the Titan, Styx, who was a daughter of Oceanus. She was among the few Titans who sided with Zeus in his attempt to take the rulership from his father, Kronos. Granted, she did this partly to get back at her older sister, Themis, who was Zeus' first wife. Styx thought Themis was faithless to Zeus for not sticking by him during his siege of power. But Styx also never admitted she had feelings for Zeus.

When this revolt happened, Styx appeared to Zeus in secrecy to let Zeus and his generals know of the Titans' plans. Styx only asked Zeus for one thing in exchange for her espionage: To protect her from the Titans when they eventually found her out. Zeus tells her that she has his word to keep her safe.

Eventually, Zeus destroyed Kronos and in order that his father would never rise again, he cut him into several pieces and spread them everywhere to be consumed. Some to the sea and some to monsters. In the middle of spreading the dead flesh of Kronos across the world so that he might never rise again, three women made of shadow appeared, called the Erinyes. They were furious over the death of Kronos because they feared Olympus would become unstable again. But the Erinyes knew that Zeus must have had his a source of information from somewhere to anticipate Krono's plans. Zeus would not tell.

The Erinyes did not need Zeus to say anything. In their shadowy forms, they jumped into his heart and mind to find who assisted him. They immediately flew towards Styx and tortured her with nightmares and blindness. One of the Erinyes, Megaera, went to her cousin, Atropos, one of the Moirae, and told her to snip the unbreakable thread of life of Styx. Atropos did not know how to do this, so Megaera took Atropos' shears and dipped them in one of the rivers in the Underworld. She brought it back and snipped the thread of Styx, and Styx collapsed dead.

Zeus was angry at such cruelty by the Erinyes, but he was more angry at himself for failing to protect Styx when he gave her his word. He also knew that lashing out at the Erinyes or the Moirae would be countered with their own threat to snip Zeus' thread of life.

Megaera feigned concern when she asked why he looked so sad. They

150

already had the revenge they wanted. As long as he was able to keep peace in Olympus, then the Erinyes had no further grudge. After all, Zeus may have been an adversary; but Styx had committed treachery.

"I have failed to keep my promise to protect Styx. My word is supposed to be my bond. Without such oaths, this realm will descend into chaos." Zeus looked more solemn than sad, but the Erinyes knew he was completely correct.

"Would you believe that to be true?" asked another woman. Standing before Zeus were three other women. They all looked alike except one was a young maiden, one had the face of a young mother and one was a grand sage. They were the Moirae, weavers of life. The one who spoke was the oldest of them all and carried a pair of heavy shears.

"Yes, I believe that to be true," said Zeus. The Moirae huddled amongst themselves and then turned around to face him.

"Would you pay that price with your life and power?" asked the youngest.

"Yes, I would. And the rest of Olympus should, too," said Zeus. He had taken the rulership of Olympus by force, and now was the time for him to act as king.

"Very well," said the oldest one, Atropos. "We will strike a bargain with you. If the oaths you or any god make are so important that you are willing to leave your life and power behind, then you must make a point to remember Styx and what you failed to do. And if that oath is not kept, you forfeit your power and your life. Forever."

"If I may, elder one," said Zeus respectfully, choosing his words carefully. "If you wish to make us keep such an oath, then you too must swear that your shears will never touch the thread of a god or a titan. Constant death in Olympus will not make this place stable."

"We will revisit this in time. Securing that would mean the rulership will never change, even if you become tyrannical," said Atropos. "But it is in our best interest for the constant death to stop in Olympus."

Zeus took the body of Styx and buried her in the largest river in the Underworld, that river bears her name to this day. This explains why oaths to the river Styx are not meant to be broken. It also explains why there was so much death before Zeus' rule, from gods and titans fighting and they "seem" to be immortal now.

So gods swearing an oath by the river Styx better be prepared to follow through, no matter how much they do not like it. Otherwise their death is their own fault.

150

HERMES THE CATTLE THIEF

According to legends on Earth, when Hermes was still in swaddling clothes as a babe, he crawled out of his mother's arms and took Apollo's sacred cattle. When Apollo accused the infant Hermes of taking the cattle, Hermes gave him a handcrafted lyre and Apollo dropped his anger over the whole thing.

I asked my father about this, and he said it was somewhat true. The age was not quite right and there were a few details missing. He did not do this just to be precocious

"First of all," said Hermes. "You talk about the sacred cow. That cow wasn't sacred at all. Apollo was a teenager and before he was allowed to deal with horses, he had to learn to deal with other farm animals like goats and pigs. Taking care of cattle before he was allowed to move on to horses annoyed him.

"I did not know all that at the time, because hey, I was only eight years old. I thought, "Maybe if there were no cattle around, he would be forced to take care of horses and he will get what he wants! Right?'

"So one night when Apollo had his cattle locked up, I unlocked the barn (by the way, Apollo REALLY did not do a good job of this) and took the cattle to a cave. I was pretty proud of myself and thought Apollo will be happy to take care of horses now.

"His reaction was not what I expected. He was pretty angry when he discovered someone had taken his cattle. I also knew that one of Apollo's major powers is his ability to get the truth from anybody. He looked at me and I knew that he knew.

"He went up to my mother and yelled at her for what I did. He was upset and I did not know why. My mother became defensive, not knowing anything saying I had been home all night. Apollo looked at her and then looked at me. I knew that he knew that she did not know anything about what I did... (hopefully that made sense).

"Apollo got in my face and demanded to know where the cattle were. He made me walk with him to the caves where I had stored the cattle. As a kid, this was the longest walk of shame. The cows were all fine; they seemed to be happily grazing on cave moss. (The fact that cows don't care if it's grass or moss disturbs me a bit.)

"When Apollo asked me to explain myself, I froze. I just did not know what to say, so I just fidgeted uncomfortably with a toy I had been working on. Apollo looked at what was in my hands. I was actually trying to make a bow with multiple strings so I could shoot several arrows at once. Apollo took it out of my hands and plucked each string. Each one made a different musical note, and he smiled.

"'Listen, if I can keep this thing, we will call it fair and settled,' said Apollo.

150

I was not particularly attached to my toy that didn't even work the way I wanted it to. So if this got me out of trouble, I was happy for him to take it."

I smiled. "Dad, the part where you froze and had nothing to say does not sound like you at all."

"Well, it was the first time I had ever been caught. I did not know how to react. So it sounds exactly like me because I was there," said my dad with a smile and a wink.

CLYTIE THE DEVOTED

Most gods like fanatical devotion. But we draw the line at stalkers.

Clytie was a nymph of some sort, possibly of the woods or of the sea; but none of us knew for sure. She looked more unlike a nymph than even mortals. No one could explain why her body was completely swollen, including her face. Her swelling had the unfortunate effect of making her eyes look exceptionally beady and her nose pig-like. This was not a matter of simply having extra curves on her figure because personally, I like ample features. No, this was a matter of complete bodily disproportion. Unfortunately, there were not many physicians who could diagnose this easily. But there was a god who could do wondrous healing: Apollo.

Apollo was actually somewhat repulsed when he saw Clytie, but he was too polite to let it show. He looked her over and found that her swelling was an allergic reaction to bees. The place where she lived was a heavily wooded area full of

150

stinging insects. Apollo simply asked her to move herself away from the place. However, Clytie needed some reassurance. She revealed herself as a nymph of the water AND the wood so she simply cannot just move. The tree from which she comes is a huge tree with roots and dangle into the flowing river.

Apollo called upon one of his sons, Aristaeus, to handle the bees. Artisteus climbed the branches of Clytie's tree, grabbed the hives and stuffed them into his beard. The swelling on Clytie's face and body went down a little and she was in less pain. However, her face still had beady eyes and a pig-like nose. Still, Clytie was eternally grateful.

Every morning, Clytie now made a point to greet Apollo in the sky. Apollo waved back each time. After a few days, Clytie greeted Apollo in the early dawn, drawing closer and closer to his golden palace. Soon she greeted Apollo at his chariot before he left to travel. Clytie would fawn over him, giving him flowers and other small gifts.

One time he arrived at his sun chariot, ready to take off when he saw it was decorated with lots of flowers. She even spelled "From your Clytie" in flowers in front of his chariot. Apollo removed all the flowers because they would burn from the flames of his fiery steeds. The next day, he found even MORE flowers in the chariot.

One night after sunset, he arrived at the sun palace to find Clytie going through his dirty tunics, sniffing them. Apollo asked what she was doing, to which Clytie responded she wanted to make sure they were clean. In any case, she made him a new tunic, dyed indigo and urged him to try it on in front of her. Apollo is usually very proud of his body but he suddenly felt very shy. In fact, he walked away to try this tunic on, only to find that this did not cover very much of him at all. Apollo felt uncomfortable and urged Clytie to leave.

"Are you not appreciative for all that I do for you, my Lord?" asked Clytie.

"I must sleep so I can get up early to drive the sun chariot," said Apollo.

"Maybe I can keep you company as you sleep so you will not be alone," said Clytie suggestively.

"That will not be necessary," said Apollo and again asked her to leave. Once Clytie left the palace completely, he donned a hooded cloak and quickly traveled to Olympus, seeking Aphrodite.

"Why are you skulking in secret?" asked Aphrodite.

"How do you get someone to stop being in love with you?" asked Apollo in total exasperation.

"I do not do those things, Apollo. I make people fall in love, not out of it. And if anyone does have just cause to break those bonds, I do not want to hear of it." With that, Aphrodite walked away.

I was so surprised to see Apollo wandering around so late in a hooded cloak. I was working late in the hall of justice.

"Bellaramon, I need to talk to you. How do you get someone to not fall in love with you?"

"Just ignore her," I said. "If you ignore someone and do not react to anything she do, she will turn her energy to someone else."

"Yes, but Clytie is breaking into my palace, decorating my chariot and getting into my tunics!"

"That hag?! I mean… that's not good. Apollo, why don't you have guards at your palace?"

"It's never been an issue before. My palace is not easy to find or to get into."

"You should consider it," I said.

Apollo told me later what he did. He asked Aristaeus to come to his palace and remove the beehives from his beard. He instructed his son to decorate the

150

willow trees in front of the palace with them. When Clytie came the next morning, she could not pass the swarms of bees in her way.

Clytie tried each morning to enter the palace but could not. Clytie shouted "Hello" to Apollo in the sky, but Apollo pretended not to notice her, staring straight ahead. After ignoring her constantly, Clytie stopped coming to the palace. But every day, she would watch Apollo's chariot ride into the sky and do nothing else. She would not eat or do anything else and was wasting away.

Aphrodite saw her and took pity on her. Clytie's love was unrequited but Aphrodite thought the nymph did not need to die from this. As she was about to die, Aphrodite turned her into a sunflower. Yet even still, as a sunflower, Clytie's head looks to the sun.

PERSEUS, A TOOL OF THE GODS

Let me start off by saying that of the many heroes on Earth, Perseus would never be named the brightest. Athene and Hermes have to explain concepts to him repeatedly, and he often asks questions about things people already explained to him. For the sake of this story, I took out most of the tedious parts of "Perseus not getting it." To make up for his lack of wisdom, Perseus was often direct and had a courage that did not falter from overthinking.

The King of Argos, Arcisius, wanted sons badly. He had only one daughter that survived childbirth named Danaë. He went to an Oracle of Zeus, where it was revealed he would never have sons. And even worse, his daughter would bear a son that will eventually reclaim the throne... by killing him. Arcisius reacted by locking his daughter in her room for fear of his life.

Zeus found Danaë to be curvaceous and tempting. He has not had sex in a

150

few days so he became obsessed with bedding her. Now that King Arcisius had locked her up in her room, Zeus was intrigued by the challenge of getting to her. Zeus went to the palace in the guise of one of the guards and in the dark of night, he entered her room.

Danaë awakened not knowing who was in her room with her. Zeus, unable to control himself anymore, undid his tunic and touched himself. His fingers barely grabbed himself when he... exploded a golden rain onto Danaë. Completely embarrassed, Zeus ran out of the room and returned to Olympus.

Danaë, half asleep during the whole thing, was completely unaware she was pregnant. In fact, her father just assumed that she had a healthy appetite. When she gave birth, Arcisius knew of the oracle but he could not bear to kill his grandson. So instead he made one of his soldiers do it. The soldier could not bear to do it either. So the king put Danaë and the baby Perseus into a locked trunk and floated it away from Argos, never intending to deal with them again.

Zeus saw this and guided the trunk to a place far away where a kindly fisherman, Dictys, and his wife would find the trunk. Inside, Dictys heard a baby crying and opened it right away. As they had no children of their own, they happily took them in and raised Danaë and Perseus as their own.

The life of Perseus growing up was completely without incident. However, the ruler of the island, Polydectes, fell in love with the beautiful Danaë, who never lost her beauty even when Perseus was full grown. He proposed to her and she accepted. The one problem is that he did not want Perseus around.

There was a party held before the wedding and each person came with a gift, but poor Perseus had nothing to give. He was not even sure what to bring. Polydectes put into his head that there was a gift that he secretly wanted, but played reluctant when Perseus pressed him for details. Perseus insisted to know what Polydectes really wanted.

Polydectes said he wanted the head of the Gorgon, Medusa. Perseus did not even know what a Gorgon was. Polydectes explained it was a "snake like creature" with a precious jewel in its forehead.

Then Perseus asked, "If it such a common creature, why does it have the name 'Medusa?'" Polydectes sighed because he realized that Perseus was not as completely dumb as he looked. So the ruler of the island city began to explain:

"Medusa used to be a priestess of Aphrodite and served her goddess loyally. But one day, Medusa fell in love with a young man who entered the temple. She asked for the blessing of Aphrodite to leave her service to be with that man. Aphrodite did not answer her. Medusa asked Aphrodite every day for her blessing until she responded. When Aphrodite finally did answer, she told Medusa this young man was meant for someone else. That someone else was another priestess of Aphrodite and married to Medusa's interest the next day.

"Medusa became scornful. She defiled the temple in every day she knew how. Spreading her menses about the temple floors. Inviting drunken orgies into her hallowed halls. But the last insult was copulating with the bull on top of a sacrificial altar. Aphrodite could not ignore this anymore.

"Aphrodite appeared before Medusa and transformed her into the most hideous thing that she knew: A Gorgon. A woman with snakes for hair whose face is so hideous that she can turn a man to stone."

"And this woman has a jewel in her head? How am I supposed to get this if she can turn men to stone?" asked Perseus.

Polydectes smiled. "Perseus, you are probably among the brightest boys I know and that is no surprise coming from your beautiful mother. I know if anyone would have a way, you would." That flattery worked and Perseus began thinking how to secure the head of Medusa. Polydectes smiled at his own cunning and before he left, he told Perseus not to tell his mother. "The reaction from your mother when you come back with the present would be glorious," he said. Perseus agreed.

Perseus had no idea where to go to find the Gorgon, let alone slay her. He went to an elderly wise woman who lived on the beaches of the island for advice.
150

She said he must go into town and buy a new pair of sandals and the answer would come to him. Perseus had no idea how that answer would arrive, but he had no other leads.

The next day, he went into market to find a new pair of sandals. Because Perseus' feet were so large, no pair of sandals would settle comfortably on his feet. He had no leads and the one small task he was asked, he could not accomplish.

A man in a purple cloak approached him, asking why he looked so frustrated. Perseus spoke of buying new sandals so he could slay a Gorgon. The listener was understandably confused. Perseus explained his story to this stranger, that the ruler of this island and his mother were getting married and he wished for a Gorgon's head as a wedding present.

The man in the purple cloak explained to Perseus that this task was crazy, but this did not move Perseus. He was determined to do this horrible task. The cloaked man said, "At least, let me give you MY sandals. Your feet seem to be as big as mine." Perseus put them on and he was surprised that they fit. He was also surprised to see wings on them.

"Now that you have my sandals, I ask a request from you. I need you to go to North to the fortune telling sisters, the Graiae. They will know best how to solve your problem. Be aware they eat human flesh so if you go ill prepared, you will meet your doom. At least, they only have one eye among them, so use that to your advantage."

Perseus asked, "Do you not want something for this kindness?"

"I want you to return safely," said the cloaked man." These sandals will assist you in getting there. One step will take you several leagues and you can traverse on water. When you return, I will ask you for a proper request." The cloaked man bid good fortune.

After he left, the man in the purple cloak brought out another pair of winged sandals and ran towards the skies of Olympus. He saw Athene in her chair, drinking kona and chatting with Hera and Hestia. He grabbed Athene out of the chair, knocking it away from the table.

"Are you kidding me?" said the man in the purple cloak.

"Hermes, calm down! What happened?" asked Athene.

"Polydectes is going to send some kid to his doom in an attempt to slay the Gorgon Medusa!"

"Why didn't you stop him?"

"I want to see him do it," said Hermes. "It would serve Polydectes right if Perseus were successful." Athene knew Perseus was among Zeus' children and makes a point to protect all heirs.

"We should ask my Father for help," said Athene. "Perseus is Zeus' son..."

"We should NOT get the King involved," said Hermes. "Otherwise Polydectes will not get the justice that is coming to them."

Athene sighed. "Your idea of justice is often perverse. If this plan gets too complicated, I will bow out."

Meanwhile, Perseus arrived that the cavern house of the Graiae. The house was decorated with furniture made from bones and more bones littered the cave floor. One of the Graiae began to smell flesh and asked the other sisters to detect their visitor. The one who had the eye saw him and drooled. However, Perseus simply went up to the old women, and took the single eye away from them. They complained and argued and wanted the eye back. Perseus remarked that it looked delicious like a cow eye and was tempted to eat it. The Graiae shrieked and swore to do anything to get the eye back. Perseus asked for advice to slay the Gorgon, Medusa.

"Go to the temple of Athene in Parnassus," said the Graiae in unison. "She
150

is aware of your needs and will assist you. Now give us back the eye!"

"One more thing," said Perseus. "Will I be able to do this?"

"Not as you are," they said in unison. "Only the gods can help you now." Perseus hid the eye of the Graiae in a pile of sand within the cave and left. He used the winged sandals to travel to Athene's temple in Parnassus. At the temple, he saw the vision of Athene talk to him.

"Perseus, I was told of your coming and have provided a sword and a mirrored shield. The sword is very sharp and will cut through the hardened scales of the Gorgon. Do not look straight into the eyes of the Gorgon. Do not even make eye contact through the reflection. May fortune be with you." Athene instructed Persues to travel to the Isle of the Gorgons and disappeared.

Perseus took quite a few steps. He passed the Siren's rock so quickly he did not have time to hear them, and he bypassed by Scylla and Charybdis before either monster had time to react. Continuing east, he found the Isle of Gorgons surrounded by mist. The place looked like an abandoned, eroded temple to Aphrodite littered by petrified men, shrieking in horror and frozen in place.

Perseus edged backwards, carefully checking the reflection of Medusa using in the interior of his shield. She looked as hideous as described. Perseus readied his sword when he heard, "Who's there?" in the sweetest voice possible. Perseus looked around. He was pretty certain the voice was not from the monster. However, there was no one else around.

"Yes, I am talking to you," said the voice. In the reflection, Medusa was looking in Perseus' direction. He was caught. "What brings you here?"

The sweet voice was jarring against the image of Medusa. Perseus was completely afraid. He could feel his muscles hardening up from fear and he was certain that this was the effect of turning him to stone...

Perseus did not delay and in one swift move, beheaded Medusa. He quickly scooped up the head without looking into her eyes and placed the head into a bag.

As he was about to leave the temple he saw a white winged horse appear from the body of Medusa and took this as a good sign.

It was night when Perseus arrived back at Polydectes' palace. Polydectes was very surprised. "Did you forget something Perseus? Did you need to find the Isle?"

"No, my father-to-be," said Perseus, excitedly. "I got THIS for you!" and Perseus pulled out Medusa's head to show him the present. Beheading Medusa did not rob her of her powers. The snakes moved in Medusa's hair and Polydectes turned into stone.

Hermes watched with Athene above. "See? This was worth helping Perseus."

Athene shook her head. "Did you think this all the way through?"

With the popular ruler turned to stone, the other people were furious and wanted to lynch Perseus and his mother, Danaë. Hermes appeared in his purple cloak and rescued them and brought them away using his gifted speed. He delivered them to a place where they would stir no commotion and would be in relative peace: in Ethiopia. Despite being far away, they were on a different beach and it appeared that they could live life normally.

"I still do not know who you are, stranger, but you are certainly a god," said Perseus. "And I never got a chance to repay you."

"I am Hermes and believe me, I will think of a way," said the man in the purple cloak. He pointed at a woman in the distance chained to a rock. Her hair was done up in braids and her body was covered in a long golden tunic. It was the Ethiopian princess, Andromeda, who was to be given as a sacrifice to the sea serpent. It was the fault of her mother, Queen Cassiopeia, for bragging that she was more beautiful than all fifty daughters of Nereus. Normally, gods do not care what people on Earth say, but Nereus did. He complained to Poseidon about what Queen Cassiopeia said. Poseidon's first reaction was to tell him to grow a spine.
150

But the complaining continued and Poseidon decided to release a monster to get Nereus to shut up. The sea serpent terrorized and killed citizens of the capital city and Posideon stated through an Oracle that the monster would continue its rampage until Andromeda was sacrificed to it.

Perseus did not know any of that. All he knew was that the woman chained to the rock was the most beautiful woman he had ever seen. With haste, he grabbed the bag with Medusa head, pulled it out and showed it to the sea serpent. The sea seprent turned into rock and joined the cliffside rock formation near the sea.

The King and Queen gave Andromeda's hand in marriage to Perseus for saving her life and that of the capital city.

Meanwhile, Poseidon was very grateful to Hermes for devising a way to get rid of the sea monster. Nereus still wanted revenge but Poseidon put his trident down, proclaiming that the sea monster was released for Nereus and he must be satisfied with the justice. Poseidon no longer had to terrorize people and he was grateful.

Athene smiled at Hermes. "Your sense of justice is perverse, Hermes. And that is a wonderful thing."

CAENIS AND CAENEUS

Caenis was a young daughter of a tribal chief, whose body was quite firm and strong from her long swims in the sea. She never thought of herself as weak, despite that the other men in the tribe seemed to think so because she was a woman. Despite that she could outwrestle, outrun or outfight some of these men, all of them still thought of her as a weak person.

One night near the sea, she found a white horse wandering alone. Caenis approached the beautiful horse and the horse did not move. The horse allowed her to pet him. When Caenis attempted to mount the horse, the horse kicked her off onto the sand. The white horse turned into the god Poseidon and then he used his brute strength to rape her.

When Poseidon was done and walking away, Caenis was crying and lamented, "If I were a man, this would never have happened! No one would throw

150

me down and rape me! No one would tell me that I could never be strong! I wish I were a man to show them all!"

Poseidon heard her words, turned around looked down at her. "Do you believe simply being a man would give you all that? Do you think you will be stronger just because you are a man? Do you think you will never be raped if you were a man?"

Hot angry tears streamed down Caenis' face. "Yes, I believe this with all my heart!" she yelled to Poseidon.

"We shall see," said Poseidon. He grabbed her breasts and flattened them. He grabbed her between her legs and formed a member with the fat from her breasts. He took away the wideness of her hips and elongated her back. When Poseidon was done, Caenis looked like a young man.

"Do you feel stronger now?" asked Poseidon. Caenis felt her new body and how strange it felt.

But Caenis answered, "No, I do not feel stronger at all."

"You are honest," said Poseidon. "For your honesty, I shall make it so no weapons shall hurt you. This way you will always feel stronger." Poseidon put his hand to his sternum and Caenis felt a surge of power, like the ocean coursed right through him. Poseidon promptly disappeared and left him a spear. Caenis could no longer use his old feminine name, calling himself "Caeneus" instead.

Caeneus went home to the tribe the next day and even though some thought he seemed familiar, they did not know who he was. Caeneus insisted he was one of the tribe but no one remembered him. The tribe insisted that he challenge to get into the tribe. As they fought, none of the weapons were able to touch him as he dispatched every single one of the tribesmen, proving he was the strongest. They welcomed him as a brother.

However, the chief of the tribe wondered where his daughter, Caenis, was. It was unlike her to disappear. Caeneus told the chief that Poseidon took Caenis with him and it was unlikely she would return. The chief of the tribe mourned her loss, but he was only somewhat happy to gain such a strong warrior.

The chief decided to storm the nearby town and they asked Caeneus, the strongest, to lead the charge. He went with the rest of the warriors and nearly captured the town by himself. When the town was conquered, he stood in the middle of the market, bellowing a challenge to any man or god to see who was the strongest. The bellowing was so loud that Zeus heard the challenge. Instead of Zeus handling this himself, he asked the wise Centaurs to handle this.

The next day, the Centaurs came to the town to challenge Caeneus. One of the Centaurs could tell from Caenus' body and stance that he was originally a woman and teased him about it. Caeneus became angry and told the Centaurs to come up with a challenge and he would beat them at their own game. The Centaurs agreed.

The Centaurs challenged Caeneus to a fight in the forest. Instead of using bows and arrows, they decided to use axes. When the fight began, as expected, the axes glanced off of his body and did not leave a scratch. One Centaur took a net and threw it on Caeneus, trapping him underneath.

"Is this the best you can do?" said Caeneus in a mocking tone. Then the Centaurs took their axes and chipped all the trees around him. They fell at the same time, crushing Caeneus beneath the weight of several trees, killing him instantly.

When they removed the trees, they found the body of the young woman, Caenis.

The Centaurs unceremoniously brought her body to the chief of her tribe, telling the chief that Poseidon, the God of the Sea, rejected her.

THE LOSS OF IPHIGENIA

The story of Iphigenia is an especially sore spot for Artemis. Miscommunication and unlucky timing ended up killing an innocent girl.

Artemis told me this all started when Agamemnon started hunting deer in a sacred grove. When the deer jumped over the thorny hedges into Artemis' sanctuary, Agamemnon was in pursuit and did not let the animal go. He insisted going into the grove, even though his men warned him about the wrath of Artemis should she catch a man in her abode. Agamemnon decided not to violate the grove, but thought if he could shoot the deer with his bow and arrow without stepping into the grove, he would be alright. With a single shot, he hit the deer and struck it dead. Meanwhile, the death of the deer caused a commotion about the animals fearing for their safety while predators scrambled to eat the freshly dead meat. The grove was no longer peaceful and Artemis was furious. For her, this was a sanctuary for animals. Even though Agamemnon had not physically entered her grove, he had nevertheless violated its peace. Even she knew that her father, Zeus, would never tolerate a violation of hospitality. Thus, she decided to treat this the same way.

Knowing the Greeks were about to depart for Troy, Artemis went to Aeolus asked to stop the winds. When Artemis explained hey had violated the hospitality of her grove by shooting an animal inside of it, the god of winds agreed and told his brothers, sisters and children to depart Aulis, the port where Agamemnon's fleet was docked.

When there were no winds, Agamemnon asked the oracle, Calchas, what appeal to Aeolus would get the winds to come back. The problem was that Aeolus and all the winds departed, so none of them were available to the oracle. What was available to the oracle was Artemis, who was still angry at Agamemnon. Artemis' demand was simple, "Before the Greeks may sail, Agamemnon should be willing to cut off the source of his children." Artemis believed his manly pride was what led him to violate her sanctuary and if he left his manhood behind, she would be satisfied.

Calchas did not say that. The idea of making a man castrate himself was unthinkable and humiliating to ask of a king. He interpreted what she said as "Before the Greeks may sail again, Agamemnon should be willing to cut his own children." Artemis did not expect for the oracle to get this wrong or to lie.

Agamemnon's first answer was "Never would I sacrifice my own children just to get the winds to move." As a result, the Greek fleet was forced to stay in Aulis. As long as there were no winds, the men were getting restless. They were eating much of the city's food. There was no trade except for what occurred by roads. Aulis became a very tense place. If Agamemnon did not do something soon, he would have a mutiny in his hands.

He wrote a message to his wife, Clytemnestra, telling her he had given his daughter, Iphigenia, to marry the warrior, Achilles, and she must send the girl right

150

away. Although there were no winds, a messenger can deliver a message by rowboat, so the messenger rowed to the House of Agamemnon for three days. Iphigenia prepared herself happily at the prospect of marrying such a legendary man. Three more days passed and Iphigenia arrived in bridal dress.

The idea was not to sacrifice Iphigenia at all, despite that Agamemnon brought her there. He was going to attempt to have a wax likeness of his daughter sacrificed to Artemis, which would include some of his daughter's real hair. He hoped this effigy would work, because in some traditions this substitute would suffice. But by unfortunate circumstance, Agamemnon was away when Iphigenia came to the island, not sure when to expect his daughter's arrival.

Iphigenia arrived to a group of eager men. She was trying to find Achilles, her future husband. But the men were so eager to leave, they grabbed her and slew her in accordance with Calcha's interpretation of Artemis' message. After the life drained from her body, there was still no wind.

Agamemnon returned with a wax figure ready for sacrifice but found his daughter, Iphigenia, slaughtered instead. With the tension of his Greek fleet and the death of his daughter, Agamemnon briefly lost his mind unable to deal with such tragedy.

Although Artemis did not get the castration she asked for, she got the humiliation of Agamemnon she wanted. Sadly, she asked Aeolus to bring the winds back to Aulis and allowed the Greek fleet to sail to Troy.

Artemis is not a goddess that deals with oracles and clairvoyance like her twin brother, Apollo. She is reluctant to do so again for fear of robbing another young woman of her life.

Eros and rebirth of Eros

On Earth, there are two concepts of the entity we call "Eros." One of them is that he is a primordial spirit older than all the gods. The other is a baby with wings and a bow and arrow.

They are both true.

When I first met Eros, he was an old grandfatherly type with a long stylishly tangled white beard. He was a Titan and during the time when Zeus and Kronos fought over Olympus, he took no sides. Creation was his concern, not war.

He ran a school called "The Academy" where boys and girls were taught about life and love. They learned how to contribute to the world by finding their own special abulities and social etiquette. Most schools on earth concentrate on critical thinking but none of them teach emotional value. Understanding where sadness and anger come from allows us to be responsible for those emotions rather

150

than be ruled by them. "We cannot pretend to make a Titan out of a feeling and then think this Titan is out to get us," is something that Grandfather Eros would say.

The Academy is also where gods begin to discover and hone their talents. It is hard to think of Zeus as a child, but even he went to Eros' Academy. Eros himself inspects each of us and figures out our aptitudes. But this also explains why gods do not have every ability. Zeus has incredible strength and is an exceptionally good shape-shifter. Hera can see into faraway places without leaving her seat, but she is not great at figuring out deception and cannot see auras. Artemis is not all clairvoyant but she can transform others at a single thought. Her twin brother, Apollo is very clairvoyant but lacks any ability to transform another creature. Athene handles magic very well but depends on others to see the outcomes of her actions. As for me, I am clairvoyant and have my father's physical speed, which is why Athene has me work for her. Interestingly, my father, Hermes never went to Eros' Academy and he's good at nearly everything... but what he does lacks refinement.

In some ways, Grandfather Eros was responsible for making Olympus the way it is. His logic was, if all the gods were to learn the same way at the same time, the Titans would not be warring all the time. In fact, Eros is responsible for separating the Titans and Gods. Anyone who went to his Academy was considered a god. Later, the term "god" applied to anyone who had "a mother and father as a god, whether they went to the Academy or not." "Titan" implied someone who relied on his or her own strength and omnipotence without the need for anyone else.

This is why the Gods in Olympus are more powerful compared to the Titans, who are older. Gods are willing to work together. Titans invest only in themselves.

One day at the Academy in the middle of the courtyard, we found the body of Grandfather Eros impaled on a statue of Kronos lifting a sword into the sky. The gods were supposed to be immortal and deathless. I used my clairvoyance that Eros brought out of me and all I saw was someone with a hooded cloak but that led to nowhere.

In the Underworld, Hades greeted Eros' soul but was shocked and saddened to see his old teacher there. Hades openly wept and when he asked Eros who killed him. Eros said he knew but would not tell.

When each of us graduated from Eros' Academy, we got two presents: One was dinner with the ruler of Olympus. The other was a gem given to us by Eros the Creator, which held a special power to be used once. Once in our lives, we can break the rules of the Universe and do what we felt needed to be done. The wish must come from a place deep within us for it to work.

Hades went to his chambers and came back out with his gem. Hades wished for Eros to be back in Olympus again. Eros' soul flew away from the Underworld and no one knew where he had gone.

A few days later, Aphrodite walked the halls of Olympus, nursing a newborn child, fathered by Zeus. The baby attracted so many people to it.

When I asked his name, the baby replied "Eros." Eros remembered everything from his previous life, his knowledge and his speech. He spoke like an adult in a baby's voice.

As he roamed Olympus, he would see some of his former students had failed to learn the lessons what he taught them. To punish them, he would shoot them with his bow and arrow. He knew how to shoot so that it would hurt but leave no scar or wound. Very much like a teacher that trains you by hitting you over the head to get you to realize something important.

On Earth, people have trouble explaining their feelings, rationalizing them away instead of being true to themselves. Eros has taken to practicing his punishment on people in hopes they realize something or someone is important to them.

150

Erysichthon and the Wrath of my Mother

I have never known my mother, Demeter, to be vengeful. She had the reputation for being one of the most diplomatic women in Olympus until she left the hallowed place for Earth. She would rather deal with frustrations by hiding it inside until it went goes away by crying or sleeping alone. She projects herself as someone that anyone can come to for comfort. She would rather be sad than angry, because once you release your wrath on someone, you have to go much further for them to regain their trust.

So the one time my mother did release her anger, the memory stuck like a sword through my eyes.

On Earth, there was a grove special to my mother. It was very close to where my siblings, Pelleron, Persephone, Telephoron and I lived. Even if the world grew no grain, the flowers and plants in the grove never died. They had all the water and love they needed. And when the world seemed impossible for her, Mother would do nothing but her gardening and be happy.

In this grove, there was a very large oak tree. It was the very first tree that she planted when she arrived on Earth. There was nothing growing in this area, so she thought that a tree would bring the place to life. Then she added different kinds of plants. Pelleron helped dig a ditch to bring waters from the river to go through her garden. Then animals and insects came to play in the garden. The garden grew to the size of my mother's heart. As my brothers and my sister grew, the garden grew, too. It became larger than a garden but not quite a forest. This place was special to my mother. Olympus had proven to be unstable for her, even as Queen. This place was proof that there is a part of the world that can be hers, and here, she was no one of great importance.

One day, there was a man exploring the land who came upon the grove with his daughter and two other men. His name was Erysichthon and he came from a wealthy family. None of his money was worked for and whatever he wanted, he felt he could acquire. He saw the biggest oak in the grove and decided that he wanted it. The other two men looked at the grove and realized there was some divine influence. The flowers should not be so full and luscious and the plants were a green only found in gem stones. When Erysichthon ordered his men to cut down the biggest and most beautiful oak tree on Earth, they were afraid to do so. Erysichthon then seized the axe out of their hands, calling them cowards and began chopping down the large oak tree.

There was screaming and the tree began to bleed red. The men who served Erysichthon begged him to stop and in fury, he struck one of his men with the axe and killed him. He wasted no time chopping the large oak tree again. The other man feared for his life and took Erysichthon's daughter with him. The blood of the killed man was blending into the bleeding tree and the shrieking continued.

Demeter heard the cries as if her own babies needed her. When Demeter arrived, the mighty oak tree, her first germination on Earth, had fallen and
150

Erysichthon stood there wondering how to move the very large tree. After finding that he could not move it himself, he left it there and walked away.

My mother cried at first and when her crying was not enough to satisfy her, she focused on rage. She saw the dead man Erysichthon had left in the grove and she grew blood red stalks of grain from his body. The sky of the Earth became dark around the grove and my mother's body became paler. She uttered magic words of old that have not been spoken since the Titans ruled Olympus, and a shadow arose from deep within the Earth. The shadow fed on the blood red grain and saw Demeter and knew she was her master. The shadow bowed awaiting her orders.

"Find the man who killed my oak tree and let him starve," said my mother in a thundering voice. I have only heard this kind of voice from King Zeus. "Let no amount of food satisfy him, no matter how bloated or sick he becomes. I call this order as your Queen."

Queen. My mother never invoked this title for all the time I knew her. I watched all this all from a distance. For the first time in my life, my mother made me tremble.

So...

The shadow found Erysichthon and turned into the form of his daughter. The shadow as the daughter asked to be lifted up into the sky and the father did. But as she put her arms around him in embrace, she melted into him and disappeared. He wondered how his daughter disappeared suddenly.

Then Erysichthon was overcome as a ravenous hunger. He went to his pantry and began eating all the food there. He stuffed his mouth with bread, then with raw grain. He went through lentils and beans and olives and grapes and even though he felt his stomach was full, he was even more hungry than before.

He went through his vineyards and plucked every grape. Even when he vomited, this did not stop him. Then he went to his livestock, killing them in raging hunger. He did not even wait to cook it; he tore into the raw flesh with his teeth. He was crying but he could not stop. Soon there was nothing left in the large house that he could eat.

When Erysichthon saw his real daughter, he was afraid. To get her away for fear of eating her, he sold her to a fisherman for a great sum of money. He used the money to eat some more. A water nymph saw the little girl sitting all alone and took pity on her. She pleaded for Poseidon to have her escape for such a young girl should not be working for a fisherman. Poseidon agreed and changed her into a young man. The fisherman saw the young man and looked around for the missing girl. The young man ran home to find his father and saw him continuing to eat. The young man changed back into the daughter and looked concerned. Her father was getting bigger and bigger.

Erysichthon was still hungry after he had spent all the money he made selling his daughter. He went out to buy more food and sold his daughter to a different fisherman. Once again, the water nymph saw the daughter and asked Poseidon for his intervention. Instead, Poseidon appeared to the daughter and gave her the magic to shape shift herself into any animal or being she needed to be. Poseidon did this when he realized that this man was the target of Demeter's fury and pitied the daughter.

The dutiful daughter returned to Erysichthon each time and he thought nothing of the precious divine gift given to her. All he thought was that he could sell his daughter could make him money...so he could buy more food. He sold his daughter several times and each time, it became harder and harder because he had gotten bigger and bigger and there were less and less fishermen to sell her to.

Erysichthon became so big he could not leave the house. Then he became so big that he could not walk. He sold his daughter one last time and when she returned to her father, he had taken to eating his own legs and tore away at his insides. When he pulled at his own stomach, everything he digested poured out and he died.

I have never known my mother to be vengeful. I wished I never knew she was so capable.

BELLARAMON AND THE END OF ALL THINGS

I feel like a donkey, braying for attention when I do not need to be. Dad said to write something about myself here and I have a hard time doing that. I am a bureaucrat on Olympus, not a hero and not interesting. My life compared to my father, mother or Athene is not very eventful... except I was the first to find out Zeus died.

After a long period of rule in Olympus, Zeus was challenged again by the Titans to take the throne. It seemed they never gave up after all; after being so comfortable being gods, no one suspected the Titans would strike again.

There was a Titan of old known as "M." M was the Titan who once ruled Olympus with tyranny and created horrible monsters from his imagination. All gods lived in fear. Only young Eros he knew M. His last moments alive as Grandfather Eros were in his presence.

150

After long talks with Eros, he told me "M" stood for Morpheus, the Maker of Dreams. For the longest time, I thought Morpheus was just this skinny, pale guy in the Underworld. He was very weird and kept to playing with his pets. Morpheus? HE was the tyrant of Olympus?

Eros said, "If you have the power to create any creature you want to loyally serve you and you have no moral qualms or fears about taking control of a world, you, too, can become a tyrant."

However, just because Zeus was challenged did not mean others sit by and accept this. No one in Olympus wanted to return to those dark times. But Zeus was the ruler and only he can know what rulers go through. When Zeus accepted the challenge, it was a dark day for all of us in Olympus.

I shook my head and asked Athene why would Zeus do such a stupid thing? Athene quietly replied, "Because before his own father, Kronos, ruled Olympus, Morpheus did. Morpheus can contest my father's rule at any time. So the time to settle this is now, rather than constantly live in fear. He did not build Olympus in fear and he is unwilling to rule it that way, either."

A teardrop fell from Athene's eye. This was harder on her than anyone else I knew. "I will be working with my Father to help stop him. We may not win this time." As Athene created a war room, summoning many of the gods of Olympus skilled in warfare, she asked me to maintain the Hall of Justice.

During this time, Athene asked me to investigate strange happenings on Olympus. The strangest one was the kidnapping of Charon. I only knew about this when my little sister, Persephone, asked to find out what was wrong with Cerberus, the three-headed guardian of the Underworld. He had been howling all night because he missed his master, Charon.

Without the ferryman to the Underworld, all these souls would not be able to go to their resting places. Or worse, they may return to their bodies, disrupting the natural order of things. I was trying to find Charon and I had no clues through my clairvoyance. This told me that this person was also clairvoyant and knew how to avoid detection.

After Athene's meeting in the war room, she told me some disturbing news. Zeus wanted to declare war on the neighboring realm, Asgard. I did not know what the purpose of that was, I thought this was supposed to be a war against Morpheus. Athene told me of King Zeus' logic: There are Titans and gods who want to see Zeus off the throne. If he can find another enemy to focus their attention upon, the Titans and gods will have to unite against its ruler, Odin.

Athene and Zeus are known to think alike as military strategists. This is the first time I recalled that Athene disagreed with her father's plans. "Father is convinced his unity will scare Morpheus," said Athene.

"But it is not very direct and can get complicated," I said.

"This is why I cannot let him do this. But I have to convince him."

Meanwhile, without Charon there to ferry the souls across the river Styx to the Underworld, Hermes volunteered to play psychopomp to guide the souls into the Underworld so that they could reach their final resting place. Zeus was actually the one who suggested Hermes handle this. When I asked Hermes how Zeus knew about Charon's disappearance before Persephone knew of it, he says that Zeus saw it with his clairvoyancy. Then I asked if King Zeus knew who kidnapped Charon and Hermes said that Zeus shrugged his shoulders.

I met with Eros and asked if there was any possible reason for Morpheus to abduct Charon. Eros said that if Morpheus did that, it would be only to cause chaos. But Eros suspects that Morpheus may not have even done it. "He can create an army that is loyal to him by creating horrifying monsters. Stopping the process of death would not be to his advantage or his interest. Morpheus cannot fight an army that cannot die."

When Eros said this, I had my suspicions and went to Athene. "Athene, has King Zeus definitely decided to attack Asgard?"

"Yes, he has," said Athene. "I cannot sway him and he got angry with me."

I tried to broach my suspicions with Athene gently. "Does Zeus know who kidnapped Charon?"

"He says he knew nothing."

"How did Zeus find out about Charon being kidnapped before anyone else?"

"He's clairvoyant just like you are. You should know this by now," said Athene, slightly annoyed. As a clairvoyant, Zeus can block anything I sense if it concerns him. That was troubling to me. But I had to know. He might have had a good reason for suddenly deciding to disrupt the natural order of the Universe.

I did not even ask for Athene's permission when I went straight to her war room to figure this out. All the most powerful gods I knew were there, seated in the war room and I was the only one standing. Soon, Zeus stood up as well.

"Justice Bellaramon," said Zeus respectfully, "we are in the middle of a war party---"

"Your Majesty, the order has been upset and I have to know if you know anything about Charon's disappearance..." I blurted this out so quickly because I was nervous.

"All I know is that he is missing, which is why I sent Hermes to the Underworld to cover for him." This moment was strange. Despite that sometimes clairvoyants can block each other, I read through him. I knew he sent Hermes to the Underworld because Zeus knew Hermes would figure this out.

"Were you able to see who took Charon?" I asked.

"No," said Zeus.

"Did you take him?" The accusation was not very loud but everyone in the room nevertheless heard, and gasped in shock.

"How dare you!" thundered Zeus.

"Your Majesty, I thought if you did, you had a very good reason for doing it. It makes sense to me for what you are about to do."

Zeus' face softened but then it was firm again. "Justice, you need to leave the room, NOW." The word "now" shook the walls of the war room.

Athene then stood by me. I was so grateful for that. "Father, just swear by river Styx you did not take Charon. If you do this, Bellaramon will suspect you no longer." The rest of the room turned to look at Zeus. Zeus was hesitating.

Apollo spoke to break the silence. "Bellaramon, when you said 'he had a good reason, what is that reason?'" Now everyone's attention was on me and I felt foolish. I should have just left this alone but now I'm here with all these gods watching and we're in the middle of war and I'm… screwing everything up…

"Because Zeus knows that Morpheus can fight anything except the undead. And this is war. My father, Hermes, is not just guiding souls as Zeus sent him to do, he is getting them ready for war. And if Morpheus falls back, the undead cannot remain here, and so he will send them to Asgard to battle Odin." I knew that I was going to die right there.

Hades looked at Zeus. "What you are proposing would ruin Olympus and turn this place into a wasteland."

Poseidon also looked at his brother. "Removing the balance of life and death is unacceptable. Do this and Morpheus will win. Not because you control those who cannot die, but because he can make you more of a tyrant than he."

Hera stood up and addressed her husband. "That is if you DID take Charon. But if you swear in sooth to Bellaramon that you did not, then we know that you would not do such a thing." The rest of the gods looked at King Zeus awaiting his answer. King Zeus looked around and then looked at me very intensely.

"Swear in sooth to the river Styx for your next answer to be true… husband…" said Hera.

150

"Zeus licked his lips and looked at her. "I swear to the river Styx that my next answer will be true."

"Did you abduct Charon?" asked Athene. Everyone looked at what their king would say.

"No," said Zeus looking straight in my eyes. With that answer the whole of Olympus began to quake. Hades became sick and started vomiting flies. Poseidon began to melt. Artemis was shrieking and covered her ears as she ran out. Apollo started sobbing and babbling uncontrollably. Athene grabbed my hand and squeezed very hard, trying not to tremble.

Everyone knew it was a lie sworn on the River Styx. Through gritted teeth Zeus said, "If no one will come with me to take out Odin, I will do it myself!" Zeus made hissing breath and stormed out of the war room.

The sky above was nearly pitch black and the rain came hard like Olympus was crying. The pink of the skies went away. It had never rained in Olympus for as long as I have known it, and yet it did today. The gods in the war room scattered to the winds. Zeus may have been angry but he controls the weather of the world and the dark sky could not hide his sadness.

I was wandering for a long time. I did not go home. I do not remember if I had wine to deal with the guilt of what I did. I walked so long that when the sun rose, I was at the border of where Olympus touched Asgard. The only thing that separated our two realms was a small dirt path. In the middle of it was a golden calf and something or someone was knocking from inside. I tried opening the calf and I could not.

Meanwhile a woman in a blue veil came from the Asgard border to deliver the message that Zeus had died, storming the bedchamber of Odin and his wife... at the most inconvenient of time. Zeus leapt on him in madness and Odin had slain him all too quickly. As if he had been a mere mortal man. I asked the woman who was delivering the message not to mention the bedchamber or the quick death of our king.

I was still trying to figure out how to open this golden calf when a large man with a sack over his shoulder walked in from Asgard. He looked familiar in a way I could not place. I could not help but look at him again, he was young, handsome and very muscular. And just... familiar. He asked if I needed help with opening this calf and I nodded, too dumb to speak. He opened the calf as if he was cracking a chicken egg. Out of the golden calf, Charon came out. He was relieved to be freed and quickly returned to the Underworld.

I stumbled over my words in gratitude. Olympus was going to return to... normal. Almost.

I introduced myself to the stranger and he told me his name was Hercules. As I looked at him, it dawned on me where the soul of Zeus went. Hercules admitted to me that he doesn't remember a thing past waking up today and felt a bit lost. I told him it was all right; I felt exactly the same way.

I offered him a place to stay temporarily and he accompanied me home.

Now to figure out how to tell Athene who this is.

150

SELECTED REFERENCES

Cashorali, Peter. Fairy Tales: Traditional Stories Retold for Gay Men. San Francisco: Harper San Francisco. 1997.

Encyclopedia Mythica. 2007, July 4. Homepage. http://www.pantheon.org/areas/mythology/europe/greek/ Accessed 2008 Aug 15.

Eugenio, Damiana L. Philippine Folk Literature: The Myths. Quezon City, Philippines: University of the Philippines Press. 1993.

Gaiman, Neil. American Gods. New York: Perennial. 2001.

Greeka.com. "Greece Gods of the Greek Mythology."
http://www.greeka.com/greek-mythology.htm Accessed 2008 Aug 16.

Hallet, Martin and Barbara Karasek. Folk and Fairy Tales. Ontario, Canada:
Braodview Press. 1996.

Hamilton, Edith. Mythology: Times Tales of Gods and Heroes. New York: Little
Brown and Company. 1942.

Harris, Stephen L. and Gloria Platzner. Classical Myhtology: Images and Insights.
Mountain View, CA: Mayfield Publishing. 1995.

Thompson, Stith. One Hundred Favorite Folktales. Bloomington, IN: Indiana
University Press. 1968.

Wikipedia. 2008, Mar 4. Homepage. http://en.wikipedia.org/ Accessed 2008 Aug
15.

ABOUT THE AUTHOR

Ryan Omega is a native of Vallejo, California and a graduate of University of California Berkeley. He has published two earlier books: *Anime Trivia Quizbook* Volumes 1 and 2 for Stonebridge Press and also published a book of poetry *Empathy Sympathy*. He currently works with Sypher Art Studios and produces independent productions.

www.ingramcontent.com/pod-product-compliance
Lightning Source LLC
Chambersburg PA
CBHW052141170626
46812CB00004B/1539